THE BUTTERFLY CHAIR

MARION QUEDNAU

THE BUTTERFLY CHAIR

Random House
Toronto

I would like to thank the Canada Council for its significant support in the writing of this book, and extend my gratitude to Denise Bukowski and Ed Carson, whose lively dance of stepping in and standing back helped carry the story forward. I am particularly grateful to Ann and Lyman Henderson, and to David Thom, who never doubted the power of imagination, and whose love without boundaries made the story possible.

Published in Canada in 1987 by Random House of Canada Limited, Toronto.

Canadian Cataloguing in Publication Data

Quednau, Marion, 1952-
The Butterfly Chair

Hardcover ISBN 0-394-22008-0
Quality Paperback ISBN 0-394-22041-2

I. Title.

PS8583.U44S55 1987 C813'.54 C86-094602-9
PR9199.3.Q43S55 1987

This is a work of fiction. The characters, incidents, and dialogues are products of the author's imagination and are not to be construed as real.

Cover Design: Falcom Design & Communications

Cover Art: *Papillon*
acrylic on board, 1987
15¾" x 12½"
by Michael Halliwell

Printed in Canada

for Alexis

And yet if the endlessly dead were to try to awaken us,
to tell us what it's like, they'd point perhaps
to the catkins of the leafless hazel, those small flowers
that hang down, or maybe they'd mean the rain
that *falls* to the black earth in early spring —

and we, because we always think of happiness as rising,
would feel an emotion very close to alarm,
the one we always feel when a happy thing
falls.

Rainer Maria Rilke, *Duino Elegies*

translation, Gary Miranda

PART I

Family

My family had everything anyone could want. We had a large turquoise boat that we sailed through the Thousand Islands, always leaving before school ended and getting back after it had started again. I liked that. My father had built the boat himself and it could sleep six, although we were only five when we were all together. Everything was changed on the water: bacon and eggs tasted stronger in the mornings, in fact the mornings seemed stronger. Gulls screamed, the air was painfully fresh, and we spent our days just watching the sails and waiting for harbours. I lost count of the library books that slipped over the edge of the heeling decks. Listening to the slap of the halyards against the mast was the way we went to sleep.

When we weren't sailing we were at home. We had a large old house with lots of windows and books in every room. We had four acres of bush that had a swamp for losing boots and sumac trees for making soft hobby-horses and we had a large black dog who played rough but brought us back home when we were lost. We had flowers — my mother loved flowers — and we had a race car set my father built all over the basement (it circled in and out of my mother's laundry and sewing things), and we had sand walkways around the house for playing games you can't play any more on cement. And there was an old well we used to sit on, telling stories, or playing Wide World in the shade. It seems we only told stories of danger or death, probably because we felt so safe there on the round stone slab of the well.

My family, as I said, had everything anyone could want. We all got good marks at school and never got into trouble. Not bad trouble anyway. We were all healthy and we had enough money to start our dreams, even if they didn't quite get finished. And we all did a lot of things together as a family.

My mother was extremely beautiful and sensitive — by that I mean to the seasons, or to the way the air seemed charged with something about to change in the moods of the family. "It's something around the eyes, some shadow or shutting out of light," my mother used to say, for she always discovered the things we held back, the good feelings inside and especially the lies. Often before we knew the truth ourselves. And my mother was smart, too, in the normal sense, and underneath it all she was also modest and even a little shy. Until we were older she devoted all her time to us, to her children, and of course, to my father. But when it seemed to her that we didn't need her so much anymore (my oldest sister was already married then), she started teaching school again. She taught art and English and was known by her students for her gentle reminders that life was not easy.

My father was an architect who started out scratch poor in Canada after the war and worked his fingers to the bone, as he would say, and finally did well for himself. But he seemed to think that the prize — the opportunity to leave something of glass and steel and stone, to leave his monuments across Canada — too often eluded him. His disappointment was keenest when he won an honourable mention and narrowly missed the top architects' awards; how can the light fall properly through a second or third prize, he would scoff whenever someone praised his work. Late nights, long after the competitions for a small opera house in Montreal or a town hall in Perth had come and gone, he would spread his drawings on the floor and, crouched there like a child, trace his fingers along the outlines of his stillborn designs.

Sundays he would drive his family around southern Ontario and it was not by accident that we passed the places where his buildings should have stood. We might stop by a church in Scarborough or a school in King City, still under construction, and stare in the direction of his waving arms while he mentally disassembled the structures and put his own designs in their places. To stand quietly with him at these times, to act as witnesses, agreeing dumbly that yes, his lines had been bolder, his sites more natural, this was our loyalty in the face of his losing. Even of the honourable losing that was almost winning.

So our landscape was troubled with my father's imagined halls and towers, staircases and entranceways, and with his endless bitterness. For there was never any way he could be certain that he was right. For years he longed to convince not only his family, but the others, those who skated and shopped, buying chestnuts and popcorn from the vendors on the streets growing dark, that his would have been the better city hall in Toronto. It happened more than once that we stood huddled together as a family, looking up at the building known as "the clam shell," my father holding his arms up against the brightly lit skyline and shouting. My mother would finally lead him gently off to Lee's in Chinatown for won tons and egg rolls. He felt as though he'd somehow failed to persuade the people outside his family; many found him arrogant. And he found himself continually wronged by the judgment of others.

The work he retreated to, the work he eventually found some happiness in, was the churches. The clean and simply designed churches. They were a private thing for him and they never won him much public acclaim. Except in the praise of the congregations, who were secretly pleased he had permitted them a little pride in the things of the world. Yes, the churches were the thing he did best.

So aside from the early hardship in Canada, and my

father's continued discontent long after the hardship had passed, when we added it all together we seemed a fortunate family. When the morning glories were in bloom on the long trellis that reached from the house to the garage, when the five of us were walking together there in front of the flowers, my mother bending to her children in their hand-smocked coats and dresses, my father looking proud and taking pictures of the scene, then everything in our lives appeared normal. Even enviable.

But one Sunday morning — I was thirteen when this took place — I called the police to come and pick up my father. I had to go to the neighbour's to use a phone — I left the house by creeping over the frosty roof from my second-storey bedroom window while my mother was screaming. He was hitting her with a leather belt.

This was not the first time he had become this angry with my mother. The first time I remember, when I was just four, he had carried on far into the night, shouting at my mother and slapping her, because she had spent too much money on groceries. I remembered the sound of his hitting her had been much the same as the flapping of wet sheets on the clothesline. And when my mother had come into my room that night, her nylon nightgown torn and her face bruised and smeared with tears, she had looked as though she herself had been carried in some strong wind on that imagined clothesline. And that was when the nightmares had started. For years I had a recurring dream: a witch sat on the cowcatcher of an old-fashioned locomotive and chased me down a long dark railroad track. The witch laughed and for some reason I could never simply step off the tracks and let the train pass. Whether the dream meant anything important or whether it was simply a way of waking and making certain my parents were quiet and asleep, I never did discover.

But I spent a lot of my childhood sitting up in the darkness surrounding my bed and listening for the sounds of struggle between my parents. Sounds of that terrible struggle that included my mother as a constant victim. And in those long hours of wondering what made my father fly into these rages I came upon several justifications for him. Excuses, really, I guess. I think my father lost himself in the war. I think the loss of his ideals and of all the members of his family in terrible ways had something to do with it. And my father was also awfully bright, and he knew everything and wanted everything and felt a great deal of the right things slipping through his fingers. I think that's the way he felt. He used to spend a lot of time feeling lonely even among his friends and family. And that way he had of living at a distance from the things he wanted most, that's what made him angry.

On that Sunday morning when I was thirteen the police came along with the family doctor, who has to be present in these cases, and who happened to be an old and close friend of our family. My father was led away a short time later to a waiting cruiser wearing a coat over his pajamas, and he didn't protest until he was actually in the back seat of the car, his hands pressing against the wire mesh that separated him from the driver. Then he wanted to open the window and say something to the family doctor. He only got the window down about an inch or so and said, "I hope this haunts you for the rest of your life."

I know what he said because I was hiding behind the black trunk of a giant elm tree that stood on a rise next to our house, a tree that died soon afterward of Dutch Elm disease. I was afraid he would know who had called the police. He must have known that it wasn't my mother, because he'd had her upstairs in the bedroom the whole time. She'd been in no position to call the police with him holding her down like that, hissing at her face, beating her so badly she had bruises on her pale skin for weeks. And she lost the hearing in her right ear.

So I stood behind that tree and watched him leave. I knew he would feel betrayed. I remembered clinging hard to the dying bark of that tree as the cruiser took my father away. I think it was the first day in my own life. The first important day.

My father was held for observation at the provincial mental hospital on what was called a "thirty-day certificate." And all that time I felt in my stomach, in my sleep, that my father would come out of the hospital even more angry and kill me. Or perhaps my mother. Or perhaps all of us. He had always had guns in a locked closet even though he didn't go hunting or anything. And I felt responsible for the things that would come next. The terrible things.

While he was in the hospital my father kept telling the psychiatrists that his wife had made up the stories of his violence. That she was anxious to have him out of the way because she was having an affair with the family doctor. He said this to the doctors with a kind of compassion in his voice, as though he understood he had mistreated his wife somehow, but that he deserved better, and found it difficult to make the two things meet in the middle of himself. He gathered the information against my mother so carefully, if passion can be that careful, that his stories had the doctors at least partly convinced of the ways in which she had continually betrayed him. So that they would understand how it is when a man feels pushed . . . .

Some days my mother went to the hospital to sit on a chair between my father and the doctors, and there, in a triangle, they were to patch together the most painful parts of a twenty-five-year marriage. As a child I pictured it like a quilting bee made up of all the sad things; the war, the hardships of those first years in Canada, his disappointments in his work, his disappointments in his children, the way we grew away from him to survive, my father's anger, my mother's love. My mother always ended by weeping at the things my father said so calmly to the doctors, as though he actually believed them. She would cry quietly, looking down into her lap, because she was ashamed to be accusing him, and ashamed to be losing him, both. And my father would always say at these times, "You can see she's a nervous woman." And the three-way conversations would end with my father strangely triumphant.

In my father's favour there was also the fact that he was an accomplished man in his career who seemed to conduct his life well, at least publicly. The doctors were aware that a man with a history of mental disorder quickly loses that career, his right to drive a car, his entire credibility. People begin to see an unbuttoned shirt or a sleepless night as signs. From that time on he is continually suspect. So there was, I suppose, the obligation on the hospital's part to protect my father's rights.

Taking all these things into account, the hospital released him earlier than usual under the circumstances. In fact the circumstances of the man mercilessly beating the woman on a Sunday morning in November seemed to be almost forgotten.

I remember how surprised our family doctor was. He'd put his long-time friendship with our family on the line to help my father, and here the hospital wasn't following up on it. He was angry and phoned the psychiatrist in charge. We could hear it all because we were in the waiting room of his office then. We were a family huddled together in disbelief, afraid to go home and receive the man they were releasing once again into our care. We had never imagined what would happen if the hospital failed.

First we heard our doctor tell them at the hospital how he'd been a close friend of my father's for years. We heard him say how he'd delivered my brother and learned a great deal about sailing, well, almost everything, even laughing, from my father. That's true, my mother whispered, ashamed to be listening. And yet, our doctor insisted, he was a dangerous man. My mother bowed her head then and said nothing.

Our doctor told them how my sister had been banished from our lives for her impetuous marriage. And when he'd tried to talk some sense into my father, he thought he might have been killed for the advice. My father, with his eyes blazing, and barely able to get the words out of his foaming mouth, had screamed that he'd gone too far, as a physician and as a friend. And from that time on our doctor had never really spoken intimately with my father again. He'd "lost contact," as he said to the hospital.

Here our doctor's voice dropped, so that we could barely hear him. Now that he'd actually helped to put my father in hospital, he said, there was no telling what might happen. He said he feared for his own safety if my father was released. Not to mention the people who had already been threatened by his actions. The people closest to him. The people that loved him.

My mother started crying. I suppose she had looked at the people closest to my father, his children hunched miserably over some tattered magazines in the doctor's tiny waiting room. I suppose she had suddenly caught sight of herself in that same room. Just waiting. Although she was pretending to read a magazine, the pages were wet with tears and her shoulders were shaking. "He feels completely cut off from his friends and family," our doctor was shouting. "Can't you see he has nothing left to lose?"

They didn't see. There was more arguing, our doctor's voice was breaking. He himself sounded close to tears. "You want to offer me some professional help? You think I'm overreacting? Look, I just know something tragic will come of this. You have a responsibility —" The psychiatrist at the hospital hung up.

On the day of his dismissal my father promised to take out-patient treatment. He had tears in his eyes and vowed great affection for his wife and his children when he said this. His family was everything, he repeated several times. The doctors chose to believe him. We had to believe him. He came home just before Christmas.

All during the holidays the family moved around him slowly and quietly, trying to anticipate his every need. And for a time we were hopeful; he suffered none of the rages he'd been taking out on his family, especially on my mother. In fact he even said he was sorry for all the trouble he'd caused us, and his earlier and immense pride seemed shrunken down and defeated. He hardly changed from his dressing gown for weeks. When we passed the bowls of oranges and nuts, wrapped sweets, his hands shook. The old accordion he routinely played at festive family occasions remained silent in its hump-backed black case. Christmas seemed to pass almost unnoticed, there was so little joy that year. But we were simply relieved to survive it. To be alive in its shadow.

The trouble started again in spring, with that job in Windsor, when he seemed to come to life again. A college there wanted him to create an architectural program from the ground up, and he acted like a boy, he was so excited. I suppose he could feel us watching him and suspected that we no longer trusted his dreams, so he challenged our love for him. That's what it was, a test. He called us together one day, his cheeks drawn in tight, his voice forced out with a rush of sound, and asked us to move to Windsor with him. Not in a few months' time, but now. Tomorrow. Told us to start packing our belongings together. And he asked this although my mother had a teaching commitment and was in midterm, and although it was reasonable to think his children might finish school in Toronto. He asked us because he knew we were all still afraid of him. In fact we were more afraid of him than ever.

Of course he saw our reluctance to join him as a severe betrayal and in the struggle that followed he again became violent with my mother. Not only once, not only in an instant of forgetting everything but his own desires, but with seeming premeditation. On afternoons before we returned from school and on mornings just as my mother was preparing to leave for her classes. As if to punish her. As if to finally break her.

As I approached the house from where the bus let us off I learned to dread the signs of my father's anger. From a distance I could see if the yellowing plastic blinds were pulled down tight over the windows, and the thing I listened for as I drew closer was music. At thirty steps from the house — and I counted them — if I could hear classical music, loud, loud enough to shake the house, then there would also be shouting and intermittent screams. These were hidden in the music and could not be heard until I was almost ready to open the door. In the silences between crescendos, as I pressed my head against the pale grey door, I often imagined my mother had finally been killed. Fallen down the stairs. Been struck once too often. Too hard. To this day I hate marches, and Mozart.

When I entered the house I would find my father looking desperate, and somehow startled to find that he had a child returning from school, and he would say hello in a polite voice as though reminding himself and his children that he was yet a man with a sense of right and wrong. But he expected that I would make myself scarce, would somehow lock out the sounds of his continued fighting with my mother from behind the closed door of my room, would ignore the man with the desperate look who had greeted me at the door, the man breathing heavily in one of the white shirts my mother ironed endlessly for just such days as these. So that they would end up creased and sweaty on the man who was her persecutor. In fact I came to know those days by the smell in the house; of sweat and of fear, of windows and doors shut, of my father's desperate white shirts.

From that time on I saw us as a group of people moving unwillingly down a long, dark tunnel. There was no longer any way out. We were damned if we went with him. And damned if we stayed.

And yet my mother eventually had no choice but to see a lawyer. She went secretly, like a sleepwalker, as though she weren't certain if she were moving forward or back, toward her family or away from them into a greater darkness. And one weekend when my father was away she packed up the two children who still lived at home and she left everything precious behind. I don't know if that was because she was afraid he might come home and find us with our nervous laughter and our open suitcases, or whether it was simply too painful to carry our belongings from those years with us. But I cried about leaving my books and my curtains with the pale blue parts where the sun shone through and my favourite dolls from childhood. "I'm sorry," my mother said, and she didn't seem as patient as she'd always been, "but we won't have room for your old things."

I soon saw what she meant. For a few days we lived in a dingy room in the Evergreen Motel north of Toronto. I felt as though we were criminals, had done something wrong to have to be living like that. And every time we turned on the television there seemed to be something about murder or terrible revenge. We waited for him to find us, to break down the door with the green tree on it, to phone us in the middle of the night — but nothing happened.

After that we went to live with a teacher from my mother's school, herself divorced, who helped us with our homework and had an endless arrangement of china ornaments and doilies and live cats on her window ledges and on the arms of chairs. She and my mother drank too much coffee and had long talks in the middle of the night. Then the lawyer notified my father that he and my mother were separated.

I somehow couldn't believe us just living like that, with my father somewhere else. I tried to get a sense of us then, my mother, my brother, myself, and my dreams at night were full of that feeling of the long, dark tunnel.

Months passed and I slept with my mother and my young brother in a large bed in the basement of the teacher's house. Sometimes we spent hours going to sleep because we were so busy talking of our new freedom, and we often laughed until it was getting light outside. When I finally fell asleep I would have those terrible dreams of the tunnel and I would sit straight up in bed, the blankets drawn up around my shoulders. And I would just stay like that, watching my brother sighing a little in his sleep and wondering whether he felt the same thing, too. Or I would watch my mother's eyes fluttering a little and see how old she had begun to look, all of a sudden, as the light came into the small window above our bed. And I could feel, as my mother slept her heavy sleep, the sleep she had earned after years of hard love with my father, that she had left him for our sakes, for the children. That if she had been the only one, she would have stayed even longer.

Perhaps because we slept like that, our shapes inside each other in the cramped bed, one younger leg leaning on the older, I felt myself becoming more like my mother then. I would feel, when the headlights of passing cars played over my mother's cheeks, that her face was my own. There would be minutes of intermittent dark when I couldn't see her at all, just imagine the way her hands rested on the sheets, the way she breathed, the way she leaned forward a little. There, in the dark, I came to know her way of loving my father. That was when I started to place blame, to accuse my otherwise blameless mother. As she no doubt blamed herself.

One night as I watched her sleep — and I could see her struggle, still wanting to make things different, still wanting to include my father — my mother seemed to awaken. She lifted her head just a little and said, "I don't know if I believe in God anymore. I don't know anymore." And she placed her head wearily back upon the pillow. I was shocked, as a child will be when she sees the things that have been held up to her for years fall away, little by little. I remember thinking that my mother should have left my father to save herself long before she had ever become so defeated as to doubt God in the middle of the night. Especially when the nights were so open to danger and to losing everything.

So my father was never really someone we could leave behind. At night he made us doubt ourselves and God and in the daylight he followed us around somewhat more tangibly. He would appear out of nowhere, stopping his car to speak to my brother on the street and entice him back to his life with promises of an airstrip and antique cars on his new property in Paine County. He'd bought a piece of land with a dance pavilion on it, where some folk group used to meet in an open field and dance together. He said the idea of it made him happy. He would build their new house right on that concrete dancing slab, he said to the boy who was leaning unhappily on his bicycle. My brother would push off finally, breaking away from his own father, in a kind of trance that betrayed himself as well. And when we were all three lying in bed on those nights, we would discuss who had last seen my father and how he was dealing with his separate life. We would cry for him and wish that our love for this man, the cruel love that was keeping us apart, might finally end.

Those months must have been terrible for him. We'd pushed him away and his new students became his only family. They thought him a fine teacher and a man full of wisdom and funny stories. His secretary worked long hours to please him. He would still be in his office late at night when the janitor, a poor black from the neighbourhood, whistled and cleaned and sang plaintive religious songs. And my father told everyone, even the singing black man working in soapy circles with his bucket and mop, that his family was joining him soon.

One day shortly before Christmas my father left his office early and drove with a set look in his eyes to a side road just north of Toronto. Somehow he'd discovered our route home from school, where we often stopped for a few minutes by a farm along the road. Here my mother would wait patiently in the car, reading a book or simply putting her head back and resting, closing her eyes amid those quiet, cold fields while I sat on the fence and watched the horses. Sometimes my brother would come along, and he found the freedom of the countryside to be something wild, something to run in, shout at; he would break the quiet of the late afternoons with his shrieks and high-pitched laughter. But usually my brother stayed after school, denying his fragile home as long as possible, and took the last bus home. Then it would just be myself and my mother and the horses.

Once or twice my mother had come to the fence to watch, anxious perhaps as I stepped in among the huge animals, or perhaps longing to break free from her heaviness and stand beside her daughter in the dusk. When the horses had come closer, snorting, one reaching out to touch her arm, she had screwed up her face bravely and said quietly, "They're so big, Else. So big." And when she'd moved her coat sleeve suddenly, the horses flying back, taut in their animal tension, she'd laughed and laughed. "Why, they're afraid of me. Imagine, afraid of me," she'd said.

I think my mother understood why I liked to stand among the mud-caked horses in the pasture, running my hands along their necks, leaning on them for comfort. Breathing in the scent of them. She knew, that despite their size and the unpredictable way they could fly back at things barely seen, they were a refuge for me, and that the journey with my family was the danger. That's why she waited so patiently, sometimes even after winter's early dark, smiling at my reluctance to come back into the small car.

That's why she was waiting the day he pulled up beside us on that lonely road with the light fading fast between the tall firs. When I saw his face through the window of his car, his eyes unnaturally bright as though he'd been crying, I knew that his anger had finally taken hold of him. And was not letting go until it had shaken him to the bone. Until it had finished with him.

I was not very kind that day and I told my mother that she was a fool if she stayed. I urged her to leave and I called her names for her unreasonable hope that things might yet turn out all right. I could feel my father reading the mean words on my lips, seeing the feeling of fear on both of our faces. And I finally turned away from my mother looking so helpless in the cold vinyl cave of her car. I turned away from my mother. And she simply said, with only the smallest quaver in her voice, "You've come to see the horses. Now go on and have a visit with them. Everything will be all right."

So she stayed and talked with my father against the strict advice she'd had from her lawyer and her friends. And although he was as pale as the snow and desperate in his eyes, she must have still been in love with him. Or maybe she thought that love would protect her. Or maybe she felt she didn't have any choice.

He pulled his car up in front of hers on that road with no house in sight. Only the old bay horse I had tethered with binder twine to the split rail fence. And for a time they walked together, their voices getting farther away and then coming closer again as they moved along beside the two cars in a pattern that seemed to carry them unwillingly toward an ending. I leaned on the bay horse for comfort, my hands mindlessly taking out the burrs in the coarse black mane, my eyes just barely able to follow the shapes of my parents over the withers. I remember thinking how the bay horse had already lost weight that winter, how the voices of the man and the woman before me came in small puffs of warm breath and seemed to mix in the air.

He'd been sick, he said, and he sniffed to get that look of sympathy he'd always won from her. But his job was going well. Good, she said, and yes, she was managing just fine with the two children. Christmas was coming soon, they said to each other, and they both had tears in their eyes. They stood between the cars and looked wrong and right together as they always had, and it was cold outside and there was snow on the ground, as it seemed there had always been.

And when he suddenly smiled the shy, secret smile of a boy I knew what would happen next. I knew by the way the hair of the horse stood on end and by the way he broke the twine then and galloped around the field as if escaping something that was right behind him.

My father looked at me then, briefly, then beyond me to the vanishing shape of the horse. He seemed to reach his decision in that distance. He reached inside the trunk of his car, and beneath his smile, that smile of leave-taking, his arms held one of my mother's old fur coats. A coat with high, padded shoulders she'd worn in old photographs years ago. He held it toward her awkwardly and although his mouth opened he couldn't find any words. The heavy animal skin fell to the ground.

Under the coat, just as I'd expected, there was a gun. He held the rifle for a moment — it seemed forever — and just as my mother started to say, "Oh, it's over" in a sad, distant voice, he shot her. He shot her hard, in the chest, in the neck, in the head, to get rid of all that love that had always made him seem so right and so wrong with her.

She stood as long as she could, her mouth shaping last sounds that might save him from this. And when she finally fell into the snow, he turned the muzzle of the gun to his own temple. There was one more shot then and it was over.

They lay with their heads close together, but their bodies seemed to be pulling away from each other, in opposite directions. I climbed the fence; it was funny how I ignored the blood that had sprayed the cedar, fallen into the snow. I was trying so hard to see whether their faces were still alive. And because I thought for some reason that my mother could still hear me, I didn't cry out. I just said to her, over and over, "It's all right now, it's all right now." I didn't want my mother to know she was dying.

I moved the gun very slowly from my father's open hands, because I thought he might still move to shoot, but he was quiet and behind his blindfold of blood his face seemed reassured, as though he agreed that it was all right now.

I stood a long time there in the dark with my mother. With the sun gone behind the trees, it was hard to see anything but her outstretched arms and legs, her white face falling in with the pale covering of snow. The dark fell so fast then that someone walking along the road would never have seen the blood at all.

I finally turned from my mother when she stopped her ragged breathing and her face was finally without the hope it had always held. I left them there, walking more and more quickly along that road to the closest house, then running. Then running faster and faster. And the faster I ran the more I screamed and the aching feeling in my lungs and my head was a feeling of their wounds and their love. And of their relief.

PART II

The Bathtub

Else can see Dean cleaning the bathtub; good God, that's what her mother used to do for her well into her teens. And Else had stood by and let her do it, too. She watches Dean bending over, making tired grunting noises as he rinses away the soapy scum from the already stained porcelain. The gesture makes her feel even more distant from him. She is tired of him feeling that loving her is a painful experience. "You can't roll up your trousers fast enough now to save me. You can never get wet enough, Dean."

When he turns around, startled, she can see he is thinking — and not for the first time — that he hasn't listened carefully enough to something she's said in the past five years. Perhaps it was the day they met.

They walked for hours along the banks of the South Saskatchewan, leaning forward in a brisk walk as though they were in training for some future event. She had set the pace, and they had never slowed down, admitting in short breaths what they thought they should know about each other. He noticed her sad smile several times and she countered his warmth that day with a series of warnings. He's always wanted to forget those warnings.

Of course he swore he knew her from somewhere. Her long

dark hair, her profile. And when she laughed a raucous laugh, he said he recognized that, too. She didn't believe him until he mentioned the incident in which she'd thrown a glass ashtray across the coffee shop at Wynnwood House.

"It was the end of an affair, the end of university for me," she said bluntly to explain the broken glass. The wind from the wide prairie river whipping hair across her face. Making her look strained and angry still, she knew. "My boyfriend had conned his way to a Master's degree in Comparative Lit by handing in one paper five times, in both French and English, and then sleeping with the seductive British prof that held out on him. And I was failed in my third-year Chaucer course for handing in my major essay one day late. I remember thinking life wasn't fair."

Dean smiled, perhaps in sympathy, but she felt it was with the conviction that he stood apart from her past, could offer her more. "So I dropped out, left school," she said, with a defiant tilt to her chin.

"Are you sorry about that now — I mean about leaving school?"

Else noticed he didn't mention the boyfriend she had left one rainy afternoon in a shower of glass.

Sorry? She remembered all their faces; young and steeped in cigarette smoke, and overtired from too much thinking about love and money and the future. They were always running out of all three, it seemed, and they suffered from daily episodes that seemed beyond their control; "she left him," "his parents clamped down," "the prof said no dice," were the phrases that hung like blurbs in some cartoon strip just up and slightly right or left of their shoulders. Immobilized there, like a still life of students skipping classes, they had smiled nervously above the chipped cups of coffee, watching each other too intensely, wondering who would sell out first and get married, become an encyclopedia salesman, run out of money and join the family business. And yet she remembered the scene of those afternoons with a sudden sharp longing.

"I suppose I was sorry because I didn't know what would

come next. Not necessarily because I didn't want to leave the group."

"The group?" It seemed Dean was pushing for more reassuring information. But she had already said enough to make her seem suspect, a woman not to be tampered with. It should have been obvious to him even then, on a miserable spring day in Saskatoon, that a man didn't just start a courtship with Else Rainer.

"Yeah. I was in a cynical group where the boys had all gone to private schools and had hated it, the boys whose parents lived unhappily in the old and wealthy areas of Toronto, the boys who were bored and smart enough to feel their impatience with all they had inherited. They pushed dope — they carried around blocks of hash as big as *War and Peace* gently folded within a *Globe and Mail*, right down the sidewalks on Bloor Street, and in the back of the Rovers, old Jags, were pillowcases of good Columbian grass. They were latent musicians, hung around the old Embassy tavern where Ronnie Hawkins used to hold court, got their degrees by sleight of hand, and travelled on their parents' despised money to Paris, Pamplona, and that place in Mexico where all the degenerate movie stars had cheap places — on, what was it called?" — Dean obviously didn't know — "San Miguiluende."

"Where were the girls if these were the boys?" Dean asked with a hint of possession already in his voice.

"Well, I suppose because it broke so many rules, this was by definition a boys' group. And I made sure I was one of the boys; I liked the way they cooked their food with more spices and had more bite to their intellects. And I guess I liked challenging the role I was expected to adopt; of living in a residence like the other girls and trying to get myself married out of the English program. Marriage was the last thing I wanted and these boys were going to make sure I didn't get it." Else laughed bitterly. Dean's walking grew a little faster then, almost desperate.

"So at seventeen I had my own apartment, my parents'

money instead of my parents, and I was free to let my marks fluctuate and take my second year off to live in the south of France. I even sang in a rock-and-roll band for a while."

Dean looked almost disapproving then, she remembers. "So why did you stay with that crowd? It doesn't sound as though you were very happy," he said then, wanting to deny that she might have been happy like that.

She at once resented his simple way of looking at things, as though obstacles made one less happy. "If I wasn't happy, I had only myself to blame; I did very little to protect myself. Our continual state of crisis gave life an edge, and I learned how to survive."

For a long time Else has felt that Dean has wanted to make it easier for her, has wanted to make her keen sense of survival somehow superfluous. And now, looking up from the chalky basin of the bath, his eyes narrowed, he looks to her like a man who has just asked the wrong woman to marry him.

"What's wrong, what's wrong? you keep asking. But you don't want to know what's wrong. You want me to curve gently around your success as an architect, simply become your wife. I'll take care of you, and you'll take care of me. As though that's an easy thing to do."

Without warning Dean has become angry. Suddenly his fingers are pressing hard into her arms and for a brief instant she thinks he might strike her with the hand that usually performs such clean lines on paper.

"You want me to do something that's too hard. You don't even know what you're asking," she says in a wounded, childish voice she recognizes from years ago.

Dean releases her then, his eyes still clouded with the misunderstanding between them. When she looks into his eyes she can see the protective film that's rising in the dark iris and the small image of a woman floating there uncertainly. And her mother's face passes before her serenely with just that hint of pain, the small soundless reflection that appeared miraculously in the eyes of her father, his blameless reprieve for twenty-five years of marriage.

Dean leaves the room and goes heavily downstairs. She can hear him opening the closet door with a squeal, and the coat hangers rock back and forth on the metal rod after he removes his coat. She can already imagine writing him letters. Or she can call down to him now, quickly. But that would only give him false hope. He would overreact, take her in his arms, thinking everything was all right.

Or perhaps he wouldn't.

When she thinks of calling down to Dean she remembers what a bleak, thawing December day it has been. A day with a hint of the long winter to come. She remembers driving away from the hospital this morning. She never even looked back when she reached the gates. With the warm air from the car heater sweeping over her legs and the radio on she was smiling again. And three or four stoplights away from the hospital she wondered why she hadn't simply taken the picture of Dr. Dorothea Lindsay. Why hadn't she simply turned and pointed the camera and caught the woman, open-mouthed and as blank as a red brick building? It seemed, after all, that was the only way people ever remembered anything.

The old nurse, the one who took Else on her tour of the hospital, she remembered everything. She had worked at Shoreline for thirty-three years, she told Else with some pride. Stooped and spent in shape, with a large head and face, large crooked smile, large flattened nose, larger tower of frizzing auburn hair and almost no body to speak of, she seemed like a mushroom that had grown out of the moist, dark walls of the nineteenth-century asylum.

Yes, the old nurse remembered that the hospital was the first in Ontario to win accreditation, that it pioneered the technique of ECT with a muscle relaxant. She'd seen the changes, the old nurse insisted. Seen the improvements. Nonsense to call it a firetrap, she said. The politicians were waiting for that fire last year, the one set by the sixteen-year-old boy. Oh, it was a shame, a hospital that had done so much for the families of these people. . . . The old nurse's voice carried clearly between the heavy slushing sounds of their feet on the snowy walk between the Victorian buildings.

Else figured the old nurse, like most of the staff, was sorry to see the hospital closing down. She was no doubt near retirement, was in the bad spot of being most likely to lose her job when the patients were ushered pale-faced into buses in thirty days' time to new quarters in various other hospitals. To the nearly three hundred patients remaining who would soon be separated from friends and have to learn a fragile attachment to people and places all over again, the hospital's closure was an even greater tragedy. But in the great waves of controversy washing over the event no one had yet thought to ask the patients how they felt. The issue seemed to focus on the anxiety of those who worked there, not those who lived there.

It was clear to Else how well the nurse remembered the sense of power she'd won, bed sheet by bed sheet, over the many years, how she resented that her long loyalty might not count after all. She was leaving the place in which she'd felt useful, knowing all the buildings by heart even on her days off, hearing all the scrapings of stiff doors, knowing the patients by the details of their dwindling lives. By their washing, their sleeping, their eating. By their heartbeats. No doubt she was simply sorry to see the stories end.

The stories. Else can't help thinking about the young woman who had walked into the lake one dawn in her long, soiled nightdress. Her body had washed up that afternoon after one of the spectacular thunderstorms for which Toronto summers are famous. The waves had pounded at the calm lakeshore there, leaving one not unattractive woman (although it was hard to tell, her eyes bulging like that, her skin lake-coloured and tight, lake-cool, too) with her arms clasping a piece of rotting timber.

Else knew of the drowned woman from her friend Sarah. Sarah had worked at the hospital ten years ago. And ten years ago, in the female ward, on the second floor, which was kept locked, where all visitors had been registered and visits had been supervised, women were getting pregnant. It was no mystery that the white-jacketed orderlies had been bending over some beds on the night shifts — but still women continued to get pregnant, and no orderlies were dismissed. In fact it was difficult to justify firing a man who'd consistently beaten the patients. At the inquiry, he acted like a confident football coach, saying the physical abuse was "to keep those crazy broads in line."

And there were other things, too. A teenager lost in the geriatric ward for a month because the doctor he was supposed to see didn't know he was there. There were even murders in the hospital; the man with the paper-thin skull who'd been found lying on the floor and was carried back to bed to die there of a fracture that lay hidden in his pillow. The key witness at the inquest was a fellow patient who'd pleaded to tell the truth against his doctor's orders not to testify. And whose testimony was finally dismissed because he was termed "often forgetful." And there were murders outside the hospital. Like the case of the girl they felt would do well to be working, who lost control in her first baby-sitting job and murdered the poor child.

The stories. They were enough to make just the blank face of the buildings suggest all the possibilities of betrayal. The way the massive brick structures from the last century were arranged in a defensive quadrangle made them look perpetually in shadow. Even the large trees looked manipulated into their statuesque profiles of repose. She was certain every season seemed oppressive there, even the brightest days of summer.

And today, in bleakest winter, there were no footprints in the melting snow on the pathways. There was no laughter or loud talk from the ochre-painted ledges of the many windows looking lakeward. There was scarcely any movement at all in the dark windows, some with rusty iron bars, some with new wire cribbing. None of the struggle showed on the outside.

In fact the last thing she would have heard would have been

the screams or moans so popular in the movies about mental asylums. But even the most seasoned person from the outside is still afraid to hear the sounds in these places. After today, after the unsettling quiet she found at the hospital, she can almost describe the sound she was afraid to hear.

Today, in the chronic ward, surrounded by uncombed women and unshaven men who seemed to be leaning on unseen supports in their hunched games of slow chess and television watching, she felt like a predator. Among those figures in their dank dressing gowns, their pale faces obscured by clouds of cigarette smoke, she was aware of her perfume, the smell of her own skin, her straight posture, her hair, her smile. She felt her own self-possession like a kind of guilt. That's what she tried to explain to Dean, how she was ashamed of her own feelings of well-being. How she was ashamed of him loving her. Wanting to marry her.

He said that didn't make sense. But he didn't know the feeling. The old nurse led her up the flights of stairs, the heat in the old building collecting in wisps around their ankles and then gathering up their stockinged legs as they moved up. Then the heat was at their waists, in their blouses, at their cheeks, warm, stale, buzzing in their ears, and they were finally up under the roof. She could feel where they were when viewed from the outside, in the top half-storey, where all the dormers were.

The small, hard back of the nurse moved across a large, bleak room toward several faces crowding together, as if for comfort, at the end of a long, heavy table.

Else stayed behind, near the door. Resisting the tour. Even from a distance she could see the nurse pointing to the pale, swollen fingers that were shaping white plaster into small molds and heard her say, "We're very pleased with their work up here. Today they're making kitchen things."

It was then Else felt the urge to laugh. She gave way to the thing that had been pressing hard inside her chest and let out a loud, harsh laugh that echoed crazily up the full length of the almost empty room and veered off the four walls. Startling the faces bending over their struggle with the unwilling plaster.

For it was then that Else felt a kind of pain about her father, something she hadn't felt in years. She reassured herself that her father had never been in this room making kitchen gadgets like a grade-eight shop student. This was more the stuff for long-termers who were getting a second wind, were just curious enough about the outside world to imitate the gestures of life, and no more. This was not the place for a brilliant architect's breakdown. Still, the slight possibility that had he stayed long enough, suffered enough, he might one day have been asked to join the group of doped faces, take part in their slow-handed lifting and placing — the idea that her father might have one day been told, like a child, to use bits of string and glue, would have been trusted to hold hammers, strike nails, paint carefully — that twisted a blade inside her.

Because she'd never visited her father at the time, it had simply become more and more difficult to imagine him inside a place like this. It seemed impossible that he had remained here for even one day. She couldn't think how the nurses had contained him, how he had played their games of submission and given them back a smooth reflection of their sanity, without tearing the hair from their heads or hurling the staid fifties furniture in an arc of self-defence.

For he would have felt unbearably humiliated and degraded. For a moment she could picture how he might have pressed his forehead against the barred windows, perhaps standing on some toilet seat to look out when others weren't watching. Just to see the lake through the thick and smeary panes of glass. Perhaps he did it only once and allowed himself to remember the feel of the tiller in his hand. Allowed himself the memory of his family, laughing and sunswept in the cockpit — for there had been such days — right there with him. Permitted himself the feeling of looking down the leeward side of the heeling boat, the shadow of the sails falling across his smile.

He must have remembered to wear that smile as protection. He must have remembered to hold the tiller hard against the mumbling doctors, promising them a truer counsel with his wife, feeling the wind and the sensation of freedom that went with the promise. He must have winched his sails in hard and headed straight for them. Straight for the doctors. The way he used to impress the onlookers on the docks by coming into harbour in full sail, dropping the jenny at the last moment, the boat's wake still bubbling as he touched shore.

She was convinced that's how he'd done it, how he'd survived in here. By remembering everything he knew about sailing; the navigation by the stars, the split-second decisions, the intuition for the wind shifting, the strength required to win against forces larger than himself. . . . She felt a guilt as small and ugly as the nurse who had pushed past her and was walking ahead again.

It suddenly occurred to Else that her father may have swallowed pills, accepted fresh bed linen from that nurse's hands. (She would have been in her prime then, fifteen years back. She would have noticed everything and loved nothing. She would have congratulated herself on her sense of decency and her difficult task with an arrogant, wife-beating immigrant named Mr. Rainer.) Else's guilt grew larger, and more ugly. She could feel the sharp wedge of those weeks that had been placed between her father and his family. By his family.

The nurse's interest in the tour had died somewhere in Else's outburst of laughter and she walked quickly through a vast, empty cafeteria. Corridors fell away behind them then and just where Else was prepared to part company with the small, hard back of the nurse, a series of healthy-looking faces began to pass them, saying hello in coffee-klatsch tones to the old nurse. They were in the wing that housed the doctors' offices.

"Here's where you want to be," the nurse said and then

swish, swish, swished away in her white nylon outfit without another word. Else was left standing before a door marked Dr. D. Lindsay, which was half ajar and showed a woman sitting poised daintily on her chair, speaking in a soft, placating voice to her dictaphone.

She didn't look as Else had pictured her. She wasn't the small, sharp-featured woman with tailored clothes and a clinical, androgynous look that Else had long imagined. She was bigger, quite soft and sofa-ish looking, wearing a pink, ruffly blouse and a pale green wool skirt pulled primly to the top of large placid-looking knees. Her hair was in that style that older women often wore, tight waves with some of the scalp showing, and seemed a strange translucent gold colour, which was catching the vague winter sunlight through the venetian blinds. She was the type to be called Dottie, or Dodie, or Dorie by her childhood friends from way back in grade school, a nickname her parents probably gave her. Her parents probably still lived close by, and she undoubtedly had a doting husband; the whole kit for survival was her inheritance.

Else ducked back from the open doorway and opened a sealed manila envelope. Her fingers flipped through the copies of the conference report, progress notes, and final comments from her father's file. It was all there except —

Just as she raised her hand to knock on the door, Dr. Lindsay turned and smiled a generous smile. She motioned to a chair with a large freckled arm that emerged from the ruffled sleeve. It seemed as though she'd been waiting.

"Else Rainer. I've come for the letters," Else said too loudly. Without sitting down. She was staring at the large-knuckled fingers the doctor was moving almost shyly over the smooth vanilla top of the file folder on her desk. Her hand resting possessively at the soiled edge where the file had been opened and closed so many times so many years ago. The name on the lip of the worn-looking file — Rainer — made the history within belong rightfully, and painfully, to Else.

"Dr. Heffler gave me a call some time ago. He thought you

might step in to see me. But I've only just received the file on your father. Of course our offices are in such a mess just now, with the planned move coming up." Her voice was soft, intended to draw Else closer.

"I've come for the letters," Else repeated. "I have the Consent for Disclosure. The Form 14."

"Letters?"

"When he was hospitalized here, I wrote him some letters."

"Why, I'm sure we wouldn't have those. They would have gone home with your father." Her hands continued to rest on the file, not giving away whether she was concealing the letters, or was simply stalling, perhaps uncertain as to what exactly the file did contain. Her hands simply remained there in readiness. "May I ask why you want them?" she asked, cocking her head like a robin listening for the small sounds of worms in the ground.

"Do you remember my father?" Else blurted out, without having intended the question.

At that the doctor blushed slightly, which gave her a blotchy look around the neckline of the ruffled shirt, and said, "Oh, yes. He was an unusual patient. Very distinguished-looking, very charming, very composed. A tall man, I think —" and she looked at Else for confirmation.

"No," Else said, "not particularly." But she knew why the doctor thought that.

"Well," she added in explanation, "there was something about his bearing, I suppose. He was very proud and seemed to tower over everyone else in the ward. Quiet, well-spoken, and with that slight . . . European accent, well, it only made him seem more of an outsider here. He didn't feel comfortable with the other patients; I remember him telling me that. And I remember when he was discharged. He had on a light beige trench coat and looked so . . . well, distinguished, as I said." Again she blushed and pulled her skirt down to those big, bald knees self-consciously as if they would give her away.

Else looked hard at the doctor then and tried to guess how old she might be. Because it occurred to her that Dr. Dorothea Lindsay had been enamoured of her father. That the few awkward times she had discussed his wife, his family, perhaps even his violence with him, she had probably admired him, felt attracted to him. It was hard to tell, because there was something so safe and untouched about her, something almost grotesquely childlike . . . but if she were in her late forties, then she might have been in her first years as a psychiatrist then. Then she would have been so much younger than Else's father . . . .

She tried to picture them, this Dr. Lindsay fifteen years back, sitting close-kneed and motherly nearby, her father restless, fast-talking, trying to explain the mutiny of his family. Talking about love to a young woman doctor who looked as though love had never made her crazy. Else could see her father, the desperate middle-aged man caught in the trap of the mental-illness game, and seeing only one way out. She could see him looking handsome and wronged, even in those hopeless hospital pajamas, and somehow charming the pants off his female doctor. She could imagine how he had appealed to the kind young woman taking notes on his condition; with everything stacked against him, he had still managed to merit an early discharge. The early discharge that had, after all, never been explained.

Else's silent stares had made Dr. Lindsay nervous. She continued, "Well, that was quite some gesture for a girl of — what, twelve, thirteen? — to have written to your father. Couldn't you sit down now, after all these years, and speak to your father about it? I suppose, what I'm asking, is how your father has coped with his problems since he left the hospital. Has he resolved things within his family in these past years?"

Else felt herself stiffen visibly and heard her own breath draw in sharply with the shock. She watched the doctor press the pages of the file back, making a spine of the creased paper, forming something straight and stiff to support her through this uncomfortable moment. She watched her fingers run up and down the folded paper, making a soft rustling noise. She finally saw her find a note added to the back page of the file, scribbled in pencil. Like a hasty afterthought, someone had written in the death the distinguished man with the irregular early discharge had been hiding under his trench coat.

Else imagined a perfect photograph of the russet-haired woman sitting so squat and so heartless by the pale winter light of tall windows, carrying her patients within her even more invisibly than the silent, queer buildings. But instead she half-loped, half-walked down the long corridor toward the nearest exit, her camera swinging blindly against her left hip.

Else can hear Dean close the front door gently. She walks to the bedroom window and looks down on him as he balances the suitcase gently against the balustrade on the porch drooping with icicles, probably noting that the house needs painting. He closes the front gate, which sticks somewhat in the freshly fallen snow. He is careful not to look up.

Else thinks of Dean driving down some snow-ridden street, quiet at this hour, and of what? — booking into a hotel? She can't imagine beyond that, and thinks only of his wool sweaters when they are wet with snow after shoveling. How she wrinkled her nose, and drew back from his shoulder when he held her close today. "I don't like the smell of wet wool," she said in response to his abrupt proposal of marriage.

For some reason Else starts running bathwater again into the clean white tub Dean has scrubbed. It seems a distinct luxury to be calm about Dean's leaving and simply settle into the second bath of a long evening.

She waits until the water is already running down through the overflow, and then closes both taps firmly. But as she lowers herself into the water, she can't say whether it feels extremely hot or merely tepid. Perhaps even cold. Her body seems bloated and almost numb, but when she looks along the water's surface she can see steam rising from the water covering a thin, winter-pale body that seems to belong to her.

Else smiles bleakly as she sees the scar on the surface of her knee, the raised flesh having the smooth lustre of mother-of-pearl with a semicircular snail shape at one end. She knows it is somehow this thin white line on the skin of her past, still unaccounted for, that has forced Dean to leave.

Of course she has never told Dean the truth about the scar. He has never wanted to know, that's all. Or else has always liked the fact that he met an injured woman, someone who needed him to rock her in his arms, saying, "Hush now, it's all right. Hush now, rock-a-bye, baby." He has always wanted to believe she would be fine if she stayed close to him, his arms wrapped protectively around her.

That was it, then. She was a bright woman, beautiful in his eyes, but damaged. Someone who needed looking after. He could be the good man that way, the man who was not like the man she'd apparently tried to kill.

And as time's gone on, she's felt uncomfortable about telling him the truth. The story has become more fixed in his mind than any real event. He's probably told people how he met Else, the woman who looked like the rope spinner, who had in fact held a gun just like Annie Oakley. Except without the success.

That's right. It was on the train she first explained the scar. On one of those trains on the prairies carrying grain and farm equipment and never more than a handful of people. Trains rattling on through the worst white-outs, the winds carrying the snow clear of the tracks. Not a tree or a hill for hundreds of miles to hold the drifting snow against the rails. And there, on a train creeping slowly up through the Qu'appelle Valley, the only dimple in a flat land, she'd met Dean.

She'd always preferred taking trains, savouring that slow way they had of rushing somewhere. Especially on the prairies; when she leaned into the swaying motion she found herself dreaming more than thinking — she would have vague images flutter into her mind of some early tycoon shooting buffalo out of the train windows, she would think of bowie knives and dust storms and reinvent some of Canada's history, which, like the trains, seemed to be rushing slowly past, barely stopping anymore at the towns marked too simply by grain elevators or small white churches. Most of the passengers were students lugging backpacks, still curious about their country, or else out-of-work types, those finding themselves to be suddenly nomadic; mothers with children on mysterious missions away from their homes, or Indians asleep under blankets of boozy breath, dreaming about native rights.

But it was rare one saw a businessman take the train out west. The airport in Regina had shut down due to heavy ground fog and icing on the planes, so Dean had been forced to accept the rhythm of the rails. He was in a bad mood, she remembers, scowling, in fact. And right away she could see from the way he was dressed, from the way he pushed his chin out dramatically, his shoulders squared even when slouched in his seat, that he was a successful man. A lawyer, or a man moving around vast sums of money. He had the appearance of a man who wears a suit to describe himself best, and the stiff gestures of a man intent on the process of fulfiling his own expectations. In short, he was a man she could lie to.

Although the car was almost empty, he chose the seat directly opposite her, and it seemed to her that his eyes rested with a look of possession on her left knee. She remembers tugging down the hem of her denim skirt and sensing that he noticed the long, jagged scar beneath her stocking. So she curled her legs in tightly toward her body and shot him a defensive look.

That was how it started. And the fact that both then pulled out of their briefcases the same book to read, Margaret Laurence's latest, *The Diviners*, only seemed like an invitation to him. After they had carefully turned a few pages of the novel, she realized they were at almost the same point in the story; while Else had expected all along that Morag would force her husband's hand and make it necessary for her to return to her past, Dean looked distracted by the scene with Morag's métis lover. He looked up suddenly and said to Else, "You look uncannily like a woman called Sally Pride. She performed wonderful rope tricks."

She couldn't think why he shouldn't have said that, but she bit her lip and found herself stiffen in her seat. When she looked sideways at him she thought she could feel him look directly at the white blouse beneath her jacket. She thought he could sense her dark nipples moving against the sheer fabric.

"Do you do many rope tricks?" she asked bluntly, to deflect him.

"I tried spinning a dacron jib sheet from my sailboat once in my living room and couldn't even get the damn thing off the ground." His laughter was measured, spare. "I finally remembered to draw the curtains so that someone on the street wouldn't see me twirling the rope and snarling."

Dean raised his arm and swung it in large erratic circles. "But it's this book my father had, you see — there's a picture in it of Sally with a perfect circle of rope around her. She's looking up, squinting at the sun or something, and she's spinning a loop known as the Wedding Ring. And for some reason, when I was a kid, I thought this woman had something to do with my parents getting married."

Dean paused then and seemed to look at Else's right arm. "I remember reading the part that said Sally was a petite little thing, that her right arm was powerful though. And I used to watch my mother's right arm when she was vacuuming and complaining and swearing she loved everyone who got in her way."

Else could feel heat between her shoulder blades, a sensation of fear, of expectation in her chest. From his seat opposite Dean was watching her with an obsessive greed, and she sat very straight and still until she thought he believed she was in fact twirling a long hemp rope around her. Which only he could see.

And what was worse, Else could feel that this man had saved

this moment of confession. That he didn't talk easily with women. That he was saying too much, too quickly, giving her his burden.

"So do you have anything to do with the Wild West?" he continued.

"Hardly. I'm on my way to the Saskatoon Women's Festival. There are no rope spinners expected this year."

"Are you going as a visitor, or —"

"No, actually I'm making a presentation. It's about what I call 'women's survival art.' "

Dean looked a little surprised then. Things were no longer in his control.

"Well, so far I have things like a sculpture made of chicken bones that took up five years and much of a back yard in Winnipeg. And then I have a slide presentation of the woman who was banished to a lonely vacation without her workaholic husband and who then proceeded to paint their summer cottage in vivid scenes of primitive art. She painted animals fighting and even . . . you know, screwing, all in primary colours over the inside and outside walls. The paint was bought with her husband's charge cards."

"So was her husband angry?"

"Oh, he was angry all right. He said it was a shame it was too late in life for her to take up art properly." Else laughed then but the laughter seemed to be pointed directly at men, somewhere below the belt. And Dean could sense that.

"Don't men have these hobbies too?" he asked, with an edge to his voice he couldn't hide.

"Sure," she said easily, as though she'd anticipated the question. "But men's crazy schemes have always been visible. And have been celebrated plenty. The Casa Loma stories are common enough, or that guy who built a house for his wife completely out of those Depression-glass reflectors. It's on the highway across the lake from Nelson, in the B.C. interior."

"I've seen that in one of my architectural magazines."

That was when Else realized he was an architect. "Well, there you go. But these are women nobody sees; that's precisely why they have to pull apart their fences and build statues with crude carpentry and Fisher Price toys intertwined as though nothing else matters. It's the way they hang on to their lives."

That's when Dean reminded her she sounded angry. And she reminded him that his Sally had probably been angry too, inhabiting a world that mostly was a man's bag of tricks.

They travelled on silently for quite a while. Then Else went to the bar car, and he followed her a few minutes later. When he offered to buy her a drink, Else said, as a kind of truce between them, "Yeah, spinning a rope would be nice. Kind of quiet, and it would give you a sense of control."

He told her about Annie Oakley then, or "little Missie," as Cody called her. She could shoot dimes and small glass balls in midair, sighting by their reflections on the blade of a bowie knife. She once flicked the ash off a cigarette held in the Kaiser's lips and she regularly was one hundred percent accurate in firing at a rapid succession of clay pigeons sprung from several traps at once. In her soft yellow buckskins, Dean said, looking at Else suggestively in the smoky car, Annie had been the ingredient necessary to the Wild West Show's ultimate success.

"And contrary to what one might have thought of such a woman, she was reportedly a teetotaler and a Bible reader and a devoted wife," Dean said. It was obvious he thought he had hit on common ground between them. "She had met her husband, Frank Butler, at age fifteen in 1875 at a shooting match. She defeated him for first place. After that they were inseparable companions until their deaths in 1926, twenty days apart. I always found Annie Oakley one of those stories with a lot of encouraging details."

"Yeah, I can see that," Else said sullenly. There was something wrong between them. Maybe it was that he hadn't yet asked her about her fantasies, as though he were certain she would be caught up in his own. That his would suffice for both of them.

Without thinking she stretched her legs out beneath the small table in the bar car and accidentally brushed against Dean's wool-panted legs. She could feel him press into the sensation of touching her, so she drew her legs back sharply and once again tugged impatiently at the denim skirt, pressing it flat over her lap.

He leaned back slightly from the table, his head cocked, looking with obvious longing at the boundary between skirt and knees. It was then he said, "Skiing accident?" He meant the scar, of course.

Looking out at the immense table of land, flat and white like one of her mother's tablecloths for Sunday dinner, she said, "No. There aren't any hills here big enough for a fall." She looked carefully at Dean then, the trump card in her hand. Or so she had thought then. "No, actually I tried to kill my lover and shot myself in the knee instead." (Else had a brief image of the scar on her father's knee; it looked especially white in the summers when he tanned. It was a long, tear-shaped mark he'd inherited from the fighting in Crete.)

She flashed her eyes then at Dean, but instead of taking her confession as a warning, he was fascinated. Drawn in. She could see too late — by that time the train was drawing into the station at Saskatoon — that Dean was imagining her. They parted at the train station, he not even knowing her name. It had never come up — he was so convinced she looked like his beloved Sally Pride, the rope spinner.

But he found her at the university some hours later (you could find anything in Saskatoon, even a women's fair, just by asking). She was standing behind a table sprawling with buttons, transition-house flyers, postcards with a weight-lifting woman asking, "Can this woman bake a cherry pie?", trying to hold her place among the fragile issues of feminism. He was the only man in the large gymnasium and took control of the situation just as though she'd been waiting for him.

Of course she has never wanted to admit to him that she

had watched for him as carefully as he had looked for her. She'd offered to put in the last shift for a feminist magazine, had stood there for what seemed to be hours with only an occasional woman drifting by, asking her about astrology, abortion, and Dr. Spock on spanking, as though she were some kind of fortune teller. She felt the same sense of boredom creep up on her as in the long stretches of highway between university towns in her job as a publisher's rep, her old station wagon hauling textbooks from one campus to another. She often played a kind of gambling game when she was behind the wheel in that numbing driving on the prairies, trying to catch a red sports car or a pick-up with a farmer's son driving too fast, before Medicine Hat or by the time they passed the truck stop at Wainwright. In that same way she began to gamble that day at the women's fair, betting to herself that she would catch sight of a man, the sole man at the festival. And because it seemed so unlikely — it was definitely a long shot — she said to herself that the man would be the one she'd met on the train. That guy who liked rope spinners.

She remembers scanning the hall then, looking beyond the women lying on gym mats where a voice was crackling from a cheap tape recorder, telling them to rub and stretch their ankles and the soles of their feet to relieve that age-old discomfort of menstrual cramping, beyond two women in fur coats having an animated conversation, looking like two bears rearing up on their haunches. And right behind them was a man, the lone man in the gym. And it was Dean.

She remembers waiting for him to approach the table. Watching him pause in conversation with a lithe girl in a gauzy black dress who placed herself against a colour chart on the wall, flapping her black arms up and down, looking like a blackbird about to take flight. The woman in black smiled, but he merely shrugged his shoulders and moved away. He paused only briefly at a deserted table with a banner overhead saying WOMEN AND THE WEATHER, and then drifted off toward the exhibit of women in sports. Photos of women in bathing caps, water surging over their outstretched arms, women with goggles, their bodies leaning into snowy slopes, women in the ready-go position, women hugging each other at the finish line. A video of Debbie Brill at the Commonwealth Games was playing soundlessly; her mischievous face flashing a smile at the camera, then her clothes-peg shape outlined against the sky, a look of suspended agony right before she hit the high-jump cushion, the pole falling behind her.

And then suddenly Dean was coming straight for her, humming. Certain of his kind of success.

She remembers what he said then, laughing. "Here you are, looking miserable behind a table heaped with Margaret Atwood posters and angry magazines, trying to seduce men to your table where you will undoubtedly make them feel good about changing." As though he shared the joke of her role in the awkward fight for women, as though her momentary resistance to him, her apparent independence, would all come tumbling down later. Right away she knew he was laughing because he was certain she would sleep with him later.

"There are no men here besides yourself," Else said stiffly, suddenly annoyed by what she had taken to be her triumphant chase of a small red sports car on the motionless horizon. "And your motives are suspect," she added. "I don't think you're here to change." Laughing herself then, a deep note of past disappointments in the sound. Already then the anger with Dean had surfaced.

She remembers how the sun slanted across the wooden floors by late afternoon, the light and the hollow sound of women's feet crisscrossing above the patterns painted for volleyball and badminton. She remembers how Dean moved aside a stack of magazines on a folding chair and sat down, leaning close to her, seeming to measure something in her face.

She remembers looking away from him, irritated by his

certainty that she was already held fast by his imagination. Down the hall several leotard-clad women were bouncing on a makeshift stage, performing clumsy skits about advertising. One was pushing up imaginary jutting breasts, another was pulling the elastic of a bra until it snapped loudly. Their feet made soft thudding sounds on the plywood platform.

"When you close your eyes it sounds like a very unprofessional attempt to make love in a shaky bed," Dean said then. There was no doubt in Else's mind that he was picturing the two of them in a room at the Bessborough, the air still and close, their bodies warm and wet in the tangle of sheets.

She remembers that she started packing up then, throwing magazines into the boxes on the floor with a satisfying slapping sound, her lips pressed together, silent. And when she began lifting the first of the cartons, he suddenly leaped up, insisting on carrying a hero's stack of boxes, navigating unsteadily behind her. Of course he slowed to reassign the weight of his load to a different shoulder as they passed the main stage, several issues of *Branching Out* and *Fireweed* slipping out of the cartons and onto the floor. He hardly seemed to notice, pretending for a moment to listen intently to a desperate-faced woman talking too quietly about domestic violence.

Of course it was Dean's way of avoiding what was wrong between them right from the first. It was easier for him to feign interest in a woman delivering cold, clean facts about battered wives than to deal with Else's more personal anger. She remembers how the keen eyes of the woman on stage seemed to find Dean, how he cleared his throat a little, tightening his hold on the boxes of magazines, pressing them closer as though for comfort as the woman recited the ten-point scale used to measure the effects of beatings on women: ". . . slapped gets a three, punched or kicked gets four, pushed down, well that deserves a five, hit with a hard object gets a six, choked rings a seven, stabbed cuts a clean eight, and shot, well, shot of course gets a nine." Several women sitting cross-legged on the floor grinned terribly when she said that, and Dean turned away.

"She's quite the performer, eh?" he said to Else, who said nothing in reply as she passed through a double set of doors held open for her by a caretaker washing floors. The old man seemed to lean away from Else, as though he sensed her anger. And then let the doors fall shut behind her, squeezing his mop dry in a large bucket on wheels, whistling furiously. Shaking his head and whistling, leaving Dean to fend for himself.

Else remembers how Dean shoved the doors open with his hips, how he said then with a laboured grunt, "Where are we taking all this stuff anyway?"

Else remembers how the notion of them continuing after the women's fair, already established in his mind with the pronoun "we," made her even angrier. "We — are going nowhere," she said with a hiss, taking the boxes from him and hurling them with a vengeance into a small storage room that opened out of the dimly lit hallway.

She could sense Dean's anger then, although he remained silent, a tuft of hair sticking up stiffly from his forehead and the way he scuffed the toes of his expensive shoes miserably against the heap of cartons, making him look like a kid about to cry. Look who's angry now, she thought somewhat triumphantly. Not only women, but men.

They stood uneasily for a moment in the shadowy hallway, the janitor mopping large soapy circles away from them and around a corner. Else pushed her chin out defiantly then, feeling her cheeks flame redder than her pale rouge, and said, "We're not in a Pepsi ad, it is not summer, and I am not carefree and laughing. I'm afraid I'm not the kind of woman who's very graceful about romance. In my experience intimacy has always led directly to guilt."

Dean seemed to remember the fact that she'd tried to kill her lover then. And said in a quiet voice, so quiet Else wasn't sure she might have imagined it, "How did you miss him?"

His fingers were playing with the silver bracelet on her arm very gently.

"I went in for years of therapy to figure that one out," she said, lengthening and deepening the lie. "Four experts said one after the other, in almost identical voices, that if I'd wanted to kill him, I could have and would have, especially at such close range."

She told Dean she'd stood next to the bed in which her lover lay sleeping. She told him she'd been stark naked and had trouble holding the large rifle at all. She described herself as a murderous clown.

When he pressed her for details, she said, "I can't even remember the rest. I can't remember any more whether snow-plows passed on that night, whether their flashing lights were in fact blue, whether the alarm clock stopped ticking and the house was absolutely silent, how much snow filled the streets. And I can't even remember his face; it's vague and broken apart. And always menacing."

She could feel herself faltering in mid-story; the day had drawn something extra from her she had never intended to give. But the truth seemed years away, so she added, "I felt like he held me prisoner. Even his amiable red setter started attacking me. When my arms were full of groceries, when my back was turned."

She threw on her coat hurriedly then, brushing her skirt down flat against her thighs when it rose against the coat lining, and pushed her way out into a night raw with gusts of freezing drizzle, intending to walk back to the hotel, alone. But instead he insisted on walking back from the university with her, although it was a good three or four miles, the wind particularly strong over the University Bridge, Dean hunched over her protectively, pressing himself against her in that way that said she could take shelter in his feelings for her.

And later that night they made love in one of those rooms hot and too close in the Bessborough. It started when he kissed her by the door while she was searching for the light switch on the wall. He told her the next day at breakfast — he was strangely triumphant — that they had done the Ocean Wave together; that was when the centre of the loop described a graceful curve, he explained, smiling. His eyes especially green. And the way she never even changed her breathing, looking past him to the South Saskatchewan, made him certain he had entered the circle of rope moving around her. Made him think she must have wanted it to happen.

There is not much remaining between their first and last days. They stand side by side as comparisons, as examples of what can happen.

Like the first day, the last day started with an argument. She was reading to him aloud from the morning *Globe* that Shoreline was closing its doors in less than a month's time. "I don't believe it," she murmured. "Every day there's a new scandal coming out of bedlam. As though the things we imagine about places like that are never terrible enough."

Dean was clearly annoyed, because he had just announced he was opening a new office in Alberta, and it seemed almost premeditated on her part that she should start investigating a mental hospital in Toronto, counting the number of women who'd escaped their dwindling lives by drowning. Collecting newspaper clippings, counting the number of things hidden in the stories by the media, by the doctors and nurses, even by the families. "Else, the thing in your past (he could never call it death) will never get beyond the people it touched, really touched. No one will ever know how you felt when your parents got ploughed under that way," he said gruffly, his own distant behaviour toward her seeming evidence of this fact.

Of course when she said that she wanted to stay in Toronto for a while, that she didn't have time to find a house for them in Edmonton, he took it personally. "Toronto? What's here?" His voice sounded cold, as though he were unable to show interest in her sudden impulse to wander through asylums, lawyers' and doctors' offices, search out old family friends. He means, what's here without him, she thought bitterly.

When she closed her eyes, shutting out Dean's look of disapproval, she remembers thinking that her childhood was here, the old places, the flats down by the Humber River where the kids had fallen off the rafts during the spring floods, the sandpit where they'd jumped into snowdrifts as deep as their necks. The word "home" moved loosely like a ragged flag in and out of consciousness; a feeling of cold circled inside her. Helpless impressions surfaced — a Christmas tree with brown needles on a back porch became a white Buick, an old one with massive fenders and a red interior, a small girl with thick braids wound around her head became the restless feeling on a windy day — she barely knew these sensations as her own memories. That's what she wanted to tell Dean then, but instead she gave him a stingy smile, somewhat short of reassuring, and looked away from his eyes, dark and mournful.

"I'm sick of winters in Alberta," she said stiffly, although she'd never actually spent more than a few weeks there at a time. It was true she'd always lived part of the year on the prairies, and it seemed to be the cold part, for that's when the universities bought their books. And summertimes, when the book trade withered, she had habitually spent the hot, humid months in southern Ontario, sitting in the shade and reading something other than sales sheets on petrology texts and botany books. The good seasons always a little out of reach.

Of course she insisted that their moving between east and west had started as a compromise to Dean's unfaltering ambition — already he'd won a Governor General's award for a housing project in the Yukon — but she knows she'd originally drawn Dean west by her travels in the publishing business. She was often on the road for weeks at a time, so it was the only way they could spend some time together, in some hotel room where their relationship would never leave a mark.

"Else, you know I've just been awarded that huge job for the new hospital in Alberta. I'm going to have to spend a lot of time there. We're not going to see each other very much unless —"

Else frowned and looked at some point behind Dean, her silence invasive. She felt threatened by the thought of leaving the house in Toronto, the one they'd bought for "investment purposes," as Dean so often reminded her just to undermine her feelings for the place. Lately she'd found it a greater and greater comfort, simply because of its leftover feeling of family. There were still pencil lines on the wallpaper in the upstairs hall to mark the growth of some child, and the way the front stairs turned, pausing for a moment by a homemade-looking window seat, and then dropped too steeply toward the front door, indicated the patterns of a group of people as surely as petroglyphs.

Even the neighbourhood, with the grandparents idling on the front porches, the kids so friendly, always calling out her name, gave her a sense of continuity she found hard to explain to Dean. So instead she reminded him of the time she had recently spent in Edmonton; it had remained fifty-two below for the entire week, Else staying put in the Macdonald Hotel downtown, looking out the windows rimmed with condensation at the ground fog covering the city. "Horses' lungs freeze in that kind of cold," she said to him then.

Although that wasn't the reason she'd decided to stay behind. It was mere accident that she should have lost interest in her job just as Dean was shifting his career westward. She remembers picking up the phone then and telling her boss in a remote voice, as though she were simply following instructions, "I'm tired of trying to look like a fresh-faced student and peddling books to world-weary professors. I quit."

At first he thought she wanted a promotion. "But you're so good at sales, Else," he said, trying out his makeshift kind of flattery on her. Although she remembers resenting the remark; her sales record was especially good because of her practised air of fallibility in a world of academic certainties. She habitually gained access to the most unapproachable members of departments with her helpless look of a student whose term paper is perpetually late; her faded jeans, her long hair in a braid down her back. Then out of her knapsack spilled the latest books from Trilley and Sons, Canadian publishers, books they finally couldn't turn down because of Else's insistence. "And there's no way I can move you up into editing right now, Else."

When she laughed at the suggestion, he got fidgety and asked, as an afterthought, "What is it then? Are you finally getting married to the architect?"

It was as though he had been expecting disaster for some time, Else thought miserably. That a woman should drop out of sight when in love and later in continual labour. But she only laughed once more, and made him more nervous by agreeing with him. "That's right. I'm going to settle down with a man who throws up buildings across the west more easily that I can sell copies of Raven and Rubins." That was the big seller this year in psychology, a book called *People in Groups*. She thought with weariness of the hours she had spent in overheated offices discussing theories of deviant behaviour and the latest studies of monkeys being shocked for making the wrong choices.

Else remembers thinking of that electric jolt when she put down the receiver, ignoring the fact that her boss was voicing his congratulations. Dean tried to smile and said, "When you finish your research, Else, you should come out west," his voice gruff and scratchy. For a moment he must have doubted that she would ever follow him. Or that she would ever finish with the thing he had named "research."

"It's a good place to be when you don't need much," he added then, trying as a last resort to lure her out west from a position of strength. Of course he was speaking of Edmonton. A city constantly under construction, looking like an earlier frontier town with wooden planks carrying the high heels and cowboy boots over the mud and dust and snow. The rifles in the racks of the pickup trucks and the leftover miniskirts reminded Else that the west probably needed wives and children even more than books and buildings, and that Dean was somehow in on the conspiracy of settlement. So she thought of the empty, uninhabited spaces in Dean, and watched the last of any kind of certainty leave his face. "You should know, Dean, that for years I have needed everything."

His beleaguered look betrayed the morning's argument when he returned today, earlier than usual — it was still light outside — his arms full of drawing tubes, placing his briefcase carefully in the snow. She was shoveling the walk and he took the shovel from her as though she were in some danger. Even though she was tired and the snow heavy, the gesture bothered her. Her fragility had been one of the first things Dean had seemed to notice in her, right from the start. It was what he had been protecting in her ever since, her apparent sense of needing rescue.

Dean obviously thought he was dealing with a fragile woman when he made her the boots. It was just a few weeks ago — he'd forgotten her birthday, as usual. So he put some cardboard boots on the bed the next morning — she'd wanted a pair of new winter boots she'd seen on Bloor Street; they had a strap on the heel, were tall and slim with a rounded toe, looking like riding boots — and the money was tucked inside. But she has never bought the boots. "I like the cardboard ones," she says to Dean whenever he mentions them.

Was it a fragile woman, Else wonders, who'd gone to all those doctors last year, a series of specialists, to find out why Dean was falling asleep and she was shouting? Why she was always accusing Dean of something and he was always slipping out of reach of the blame? When she remembers those evenings that Dean came home (always later than expected), finding Else restless, alone, often in the bathtub, one too many Scotches already in her blood. . . . Yes, it was in that tiny bathroom with the sloping ceiling, the weight of the roof seeming to bow down Dean's shoulders, that she held court. They would discuss the day's events in a tone that said there was an invisible contest going on, and Dean could feel she was winning. Then he would go heavily downstairs, allegedly to fill her glass once more; sometimes she would hear ice clinking against the glass — then there would be silence. Later she would find him asleep, his head tilted to one side, his beard brushing the arm of the overstuffed chair.

For months the talk was of the doctors; she ran Dean through the mill on that one. First there was the neurologist who found she had an irregular ear canal and thought she might have a brain tumour. He'd prepared her for the worst with a little chat of a fifty-fifty gamble with life and death. Else was pleased; let Dean struggle with that one. His Else, lobotomized. How much protecting could he finally carry off? And then when the allergist found only a slight sensitivity to cigarette smoke and cat hair, she started smoking — Dean used to tell her she held her cigarette like a baseball bat — and soon after that she adopted a cat.

Else's fragility had been honed and sharpened like a hunter's weapon. Because the allergist had said they couldn't possibly test for everything, Else started to conduct her own research. "Foods are the hardest allergies to track down," she told Dean cheerfully one day. Some weeks they ate only rice with broiled lamb, other weeks they ate peanut butter, anything made with wheat, and then Else consumed chocolate as though it were a sweet and long-sought-after cure. Of course she couldn't honestly say there was any difference in her feelings. Especially toward Dean. She still felt like blaming him for something, so she told Dean he was getting a "pneu Michelin" around his middle. He should watch what he was eating, she said.

The thing was, Dean could have stopped her. If he had once laughed, or shouted at her, or outlasted her at her own games. . . . Else had concocted one called "Cities of the World" to survive an especially long snowstorm, she and

Dean locked in their hotel room at the Chateau Lacombe, eventually disagreeing on everything. They had taken to looking at the lights across the valley that skewered Edmonton, and pretending they were in places far removed. Dean would always pick places like Paris or Rome and talk about the architecture there, while Else would say Rockford, Illinois, or Greys, or Libreville in the rainy season. Or Kirensk. That one had really baffled Dean. Why Kirensk, he asked her several days later, as though it might be the key to unlocking Else. If he'd once stayed up an entire night, perhaps inventing cities of the world more terrible than even she could imagine, perhaps even buying the tickets from a travel agent and taking her there, things might have been different.

But instead he went along with it, even the cocktail party to which she wore a nightgown, swearing it was all the rage. Telling him that at least she'd be ready for bed before he was.

But the worst was the scene with the endocrinologist. At first even Else thought he might be on to something — low blood sugar. She tested out abnormally low — the graph didn't even rise when they gave her the sweet stuff to drink. She read in a book later that it was a graph typical of women bored or unhappy with their lives.

Dean had come with her that day; he wrinkled his nose when they suggested a special diet for Else. He must have been desperate by that point to simply eat out. But it all blew up in their faces when the questions came up about a history of diabetes in Else's family.

She turned to the doctor, a young fellow with a wheedling American accent, no doubt at the university hospital for research in his field. "Well my parents weren't alive that long. It's hard to tell."

"What was the cause of their. . . passing away?"

"Natural causes," she said, in that tone Dean had come to know only too well. It was a tone she used when someone was tromping on her territory.

Dean yawned once then, in self-defence, and mumbled

"murder-suicide" indistinctly through his beard as an explanation.

Then the young doctor changed tack entirely. Offered her an open prescription to valium and made some remarks to Dean about protecting her. Of course that was an open invitation to Else, the signal she'd been waiting for. She called him a "psychological hoodlum" among other things, and asked him whether happiness was known to run in families, too, or whether the stigma was just for unhappy people. Then she said he didn't have the training to be insulting her. Shouted at him as a parting shot, "Stick to the glands!"

Of course the most hopeless part was that Dean thought he was her knight in shining armour when he phoned the guy up the next day and told him to lay off the psychology stuff. He was an endocrinologist, after all. His wife was fine, just fine.

Which was, of course, just the thing Else wanted to hear him say. So she could repeat it back to him.

But she took him to task for calling her his wife. "Why did you tell the creep we were married?" She remembers Dean's hands were shaking slightly, a dark smudge of hair on his forehead was wet with perspiration.

Dean turned away abruptly, hunching his shoulders as though he might be angry. She hoped in that moment for a confrontation. Finally they would settle the thing she had been urging him to face for years. But no, she could see he was just ashamed.

It was then he should have seen she was neither a fragile woman nor in need of any sort of protection. And then perhaps she might have acknowledged the way he'd always wanted to marry her. Right from the start.

Else thinks of Dean proposing in the snow, leaning forward like that, his eyes unnaturally bright, his focusing suddenly on the bright object of his desires — on the object — as if today he momentarily forgot how long he'd been looking beyond Else, at a rope spinner with a strong right arm, at a woman who'd shot her own knee in an attempt to set things right. It was only when Else started looking to herself for her own happiness, moving away from Dean into a world of her own, that he seemed to recognize her. She could see that he was tiring of wanting to lay claim to her.

It is a bad habit, she thinks, this habit of lying to Dean. She thinks of herself turning away from him, running into the house, shouting over her shoulder, "I forgot, the bath water's on. Overflowing!" She remembers taking the steps two at a time, turning the taps on full blast, the hot water rising too slowly. Marriage would only be more of the same, she thought grimly. Dean would never want the real things, only a part of the truth at a time.

Dean followed her at a distance, taking her mad flight into the house to be a kind of happiness. He was no doubt expecting her answer to fit his sense of occasion; she could hear him whistling from the kitchen where he filled the two tumblers with Scotch, the ice clinking against the glass as he carried them to the woman who would be his wife.

He washed her like a husband then, and she felt shivery and sad as his hands played eagerly over the soapy surfaces of shoulder and collarbone, staying on one breast (he held his breath there, and there), then moving to the other. Running his fingers around the dark brown nipples. Seemingly bemused, as on the night he'd met her, by his sudden impulse of being close.

He soaped one foot then, looking longingly down her right leg to where the water lapped against her dark nest of hair. Then lathered the other, his hands warm and sure. And although her skin tingled, a small arch of feeling curving inside her thighs, pressing behind her pubic bone, she still said nothing of marriage. She was thinking of the drowned woman.

She thought of how it was all the same for women, that they never had the choice to break things apart like that. In the month they bled for the first time they could imagine all the rest, becoming mothers, grandmothers, and could already feel the fear of their children dying. Marriage was never anything separate from the rest of the guilt and the blaming; she and all the women heading somewhere into the past had been embracing all, clutching everything close to them as though it mattered. They grasped at senseless strains of music, they held onto memories as firmly as they held snow shovels and hot-water faucets. And for this closeness to the surface of things, they were thought foolish, weak-minded, unfaithful. Except when they were needed.

Else looked up at Dean, who suddenly loomed as large as a cathedral-sized poster of Lenin in Red Square, his green eyes and neatly trimmed beard seeming to conceal in them a foreshadowing of the future. He was pleased he'd finally proposed, it was clear. He kissed her toes; he was wearing a suggestive smile. But Else did not meet his challenge. Her eyes dropped to the water lapping her thin, winter-pale body.

Dean was running his lips lightly over her ankles. "Dean, stop it! I'm not in the mood," she snapped. "God damn it, why did you make things worse by asking me to marry you?"

Dean was red-faced suddenly. His eyes stared mistily, unnaturally, the lines of jaw and cheeks and brow all opposing one another, struggling with emotion. The beard striving to hide it all, keep the lips from trembling. And she was embarrassed by the way it wasn't easy for him, for the overly bright light in his eyes that said, "I want you. I am reaching out of myself to you." That said she had always been a symbol of some achievement he had yet to make in loving.

"Dean, perhaps you've forgotten how long it's been since we've made love. A year. An entire year." She thought of the way they'd slept together, arms slung over one another without passion, like undecided friends who'd ended up in the same sleeping bag in a youth hostel. As though it were too late to change things, the journey together almost over.

Dean straightened up from the bath. His shoulders were hunched and that meant he was angry. "Forget it," he said, stiffly. "Maybe we'll talk about marriage when you're in a better mood."

"I was in a bad mood the day you met me," she said.

"And you've never wanted to know why." She stood up in the bath then, drying herself, lingering over every curve and crevice that was fearful and mysterious to him. "I thought I saw my father today. In a beige car, parked at the corner, by the ravine. It was almost dark when I came home, so I couldn't be sure there was any resemblance at all."

She was rubbing her dark hair briskly with the maroon towel. "Maybe it was the hospital today. But that kind of thing hasn't happened to me since high school when the road seemed to be full of beige Corvairs with men behind the wheel looking desperate. But I got that same anxious feeling I used to get by the bus stop, when twenty minutes seemed such a long time to wait because every passing car could have been my father. All the other kids were flirting and telling jokes, and I was always afraid of the next thing that would happen."

Dean merely said, "What's this got to do with your father?" and the bath became a huge body of water between them. Separating them.

One tear for her father and the drowned woman runs slightly down Else's cheek and into the water lapping at chin height. She thinks of the difference between heading for the front gates of the hospital, across the clanging streetcar lines, toward the run-down houses with cats and children on their front steps, and walking into the infinite quiet of the water. And for some reason then she thinks of drowning as a woman's way of admitting defeat. Men, it seems to her, choose differently to end things. Using hard surfaces, leaving marks. Their deaths are to be remembered.

Else thinks of all the women who might have been stopped by some stout hospital attendant after years of dreaming of death. Who might have never reached the water. The water that was calm and still today, with a kind of scum frozen into the lake's chill edges. She remembers how she walked along the shore, standing near the water and looking back to the cluster of brick buildings, the flat shadow walking beside her startling her. The dark outline of a woman in a long coat and flying shawl seeming not unlike the shape of a drowned woman cast up on the rocks.

She looks hard at the wrinkled skin of her fingertips, at the goose flesh on her arms when she raises them out of the water, and realizes she is cold.

PART III

The Butterfly Chair

When Else awakes she is in the butterfly chair, covered scantily with a blanket. It gave her some comfort at three in the morning when she had dragged the chair triumphantly from its banishment in the cellar to know that Dean hated it, probably for its strong sentimental value. For a long time they have been waging their war; his suspiciously white Flacetti rugs versus the horsehair couch found rotting in the back yard, newly recovered in a large floral pattern Dean says looks like his grandmother's curtains (that is not an insult to Else, but reassuring). His cool tubular-steel chairs pitted against her old brass lamps, carried home by hand from the Sally Ann. The only thing he has ever acknowledged in her love of the butterfly chair is the beautiful shape given it by a designer named Hardoy, and that at the time her father had first brought it home, early in the fifties, it had spoken of the future. But that one should want to hold on to an object almost thirty years later, that is something that baffles Dean.

For Else, the fact that the yellow canvas is charred with dirt and that the rusted black frame is showing through the frayed corners is a positive reminder that she is part of a struggle against the ending of things. But Dean has always liked a quick turnover of things so new they could never impart any kind of history. Scarcely even any present tense.

The house is still dark and there is a radio playing somewhere off in another room, a radio that might have been on for days. The bedside lamp is flickering, as though the bulb is about to burn out. She sees the manila envelope from the hospital on the floor, the Form 14 and conference report spread around her chair. Apparently she has kept an uneasy vigil, reading the letters many times; she can still feel the tension in her arms, simply from holding the slight sheets of paper that have remained in her hands while sleeping. And she is still frowning from watching the snow fall into the brightly lit street, the hard lines in her face resisting the call to sleep.

She remembers thinking that if she were to sleep she would not remember the important things, that it is already late in the winter, that this snowstorm would probably be the last before spring. She might awake and never remember the now-abandoned fortress of the Shoreline Hospital, or the old farmhouse in Paine County where her father had taken a room for a time apart from his family. And it seems important to recall her father's loneliness; how he withdrew from the empty house in Toronto after the separation, finding some small comfort in an anonymous place at a stranger's table, and a bed, carefully made up, the sheets thick and taut.

She found the address of a Mrs. Lashke in a file at the lawyer's, with several receipts attached, one for ten dollars, another for twelve. He allegedly owed two weeks' rent at the time of his death. In her almost illegible handwriting on the back of the receipts, the landlady blamed him for not giving her a months' notice, as agreed. Her logic was infallible, Else thinks. The woman also mentioned a key he never returned, again stating he was responsible for changing the locks on the house when he misplaced his key.

She had obviously never imagined that he would lose his key by leaving it in a snowbank on a road north of Toronto along with nine or ten bullets, a victim, and his own life. The landlady describes the house they renovated, she and her husband, for the purpose of renting rooms. "He was the first man we rented a room to, he seemed such a respectable man, and now I am so frightened I do not think I can keep a stranger in the house for the rest of my life. Five rooms above us are empty. I still seem to hear him coming in and going upstairs in the middle of the night the way he used to."

The fact that he came in at night did not surprise Else; one of the letters explained this. It was a letter from the janitor at the college, a black man named Hamilton who used to mop the floors in the college late at night and always found "Mr. Rainer roaming about the classroom or sitting alone in his office." He said he could see her father was a troubled man, and that he was sorry he didn't say something to him, to help him. "But I always liked him," the letter read. "He liked to do things right. And it didn't seem right to me what he did at the end, but I knew it had to be something terrible that would make him do that . . . with his wife and everything. She came with him once to the college, your mother did. And I remember how he was with her, proud and unsure, all at once."

Hamilton described himself as the token black the college had hired to keep the local blacks from looting and vandalizing the college. "Cause I lived just down the block in the rooming house, they knew I'd talk to my friends and tell them to keep my job for me," he wrote. "My job hasn't changed that much, I suppose. I'm an ordained minister at the Grace Church now, with a small congregation that meets over in the town of Wilkesport. And I've often prayed for your father. Often." The letter is signed "Reverend G. Hamilton."

The other letter is from a teacher who has told Else he was a close friend of her father's. It claims he went each day at precisely noon with her father to Finkle's, the drug store at the corner, one of those fifties' places with a big neon sign of a dixie cup pouring something pink. There they apparently had sodas, twirling like school kids on the stools at the counter, laughing about the things that kept people alive in the worst times. Apparently this rather pompous Brit and her father had talked about their high times in the war.

This Mr. Dalworth said that he thought the war was the thing that finally killed her father. Although he didn't explain that.

He has a great respect for her father, even yet, he writes, because he was a man with ideas and wanted to design a large communal residence in the country where all the teachers at the college could live with their families. That was the other thing they had talked about at the soda fountain. This dream appealed to the Brit; he has lived for too many years, he admits, in a mobile home with a leaking roof.

Else finds the letter suspect; it is unlikely her father ever talked of the war to anyone. Especially as an adventure worth reliving. Although he did have a sweet tooth and had probably invented a desperate scheme in which to make the eventual arrival of his family real to him.

She knows how close he became with the students from that class in 1967; after the weeks she spent gathering them together, they were only too eager to talk of their former teacher. Although their deep and distant voices made them men now, they were still bound by her father's isolation and despair; in that sense they were still boys.

"I remember the day the repairman came into the class. He didn't knock or announce himself, just started fixing some wiring on the ceiling, near the front of the room. Jesus, did the German ever blow up! He went nuts, screaming, 'You don't come into my class this way!'

" 'Zis vay,' " the voice had corrected itself. "All of our projects always needed a little of 'zis' and a little of 'zat'. Oh, we used to mimic him, saying, 'You will do this and you will enjoy it!' loud enough for him to hear us. And he would always laugh. He took the ribbing really well."

"Oh, we used to make fun of his German side, there's no doubt about that. But hell, we were — what? — eighteen years old at the time? I think for a while we had him pictured as the chief engineer who blew up bridges for Hitler, just because he was so bright. But we were smart enough to know he wasn't SS or anything," another voice said a little sarcastically, as though correcting his younger image, bringing it into focus.

"In a way he was a complete disaster for our class. I mean because he was such a contrast to the incompetents that followed. He taught us most of our subjects, not just the drafting and design. I mean if we couldn't do our math, he'd explain that to us, too. Or the engineering stuff. Or anything. He *was* the department."

"Oh, he was a good bullshitter, all right. I remember when he put in a request for woodworking tools to the department head — they must have been worth about two grand — because a bunch of us wanted to put together a plane. I used to admire his style. 'I practically invented the glulam beam,' he used to say. 'I used it first in a church, and if it held up under all that guilt —' He had a way of carrying off corny jokes with a kind of false confidence."

"He must have had to work his butt off, or else he was a genius. Sometimes he expected us to be as smart as he was, and maybe we were just stupid, but he would regularly stay after school to help us and scribble with that pencil of his — I can still see him sharpening his pencil."

Else has a sudden memory then of the soft grinding noise that would come from her father's study. She remembers the way he would bring the pencil to his lips, always so thin and set, blowing away the lead dust. Sometimes the cleft of his chin had grey smudges on it, making the blue shadow from his morning shave even stronger.

The sense of loss she feels when she remembers that slight sound, soft smudge . . . she knows why he had struggled with those kids, why he'd put everything into it. They had become his family. And like members of a family, they had finally resisted the closeness; she could sense that even yet in the reluctant admiration they all showed in their stories.

It is even more obvious in the Polaroid photo of the group she found among her father's things at the lawyer's. The boys in the photo, five of them in their late teens, early twenties, seemed to share a physical similarity, a kind of family resemblance that shows up in group photos of the war or at funerals, when everyone's thinking about the same things, and it shows. Yes, there is something in that picture that makes her uneasy. There is something holding them together, and holding them back. Perhaps even yet.

So when she met them it was as though she knew them all too well. It was easy to guess which one was the salesman now with Fotheringham, the continent's top firm in steel. The one with the impish smile, the real charmer's face. The kid who looked well-loved by his mother and probably every woman since who'd forgiven him too easily. And the guy in the suit — a short, muscular man with keen eyes, a rather mocking mouth — he was the sports writer now. The one who admitted he used to try to catch the German making a mistake. He could rarely do that, he said. And that used to bug him. The guy next to him had the kind of face that would never age beyond a certain point; clean, even features, the kind of face that's easily photographed when TV crews are scanning the sidewalks for opinion polls or filming a short docudrama on schizophrenia. That was the pilot, the guy who flies the choppers up north for scientists and engineers. He swore he got his interest in flying from the German. The tall, thin fellow with the stooped shoulders and the loose-fitting clothes trying to pull him down, he was the one who was so serious. As if he were embarrassed, even yet, for the man they called "the German." And the beefy face with long, stringy hair framing it, she knew right away that he had to be the drummer in the band, Authority Figure. Even fifteen years back he had huge, muscled arms and there were circles of sweat like halfmoons in his T-shirt, and dark wet streaks where his stomach folded over and over. He was the one who surprised her by suddenly rocking his head back and forth, and screaming out in a hoarse, tuneless whisper:

"When you're jet gray at the temples, and there are no
more temples you can find,
When you're in that other country, the one you thought
you'd left behind,
Then you're not drivin' to your funeral, buddy,
You're being driven by your mind.

"Made the lyrics to that one up with the German in mind," he said then, a jaded smile sliding across his face. "The record's selling in Europe now," he added. "It's called 'The Fascist.' "

She doesn't want to admit now that the whole thing became so predictable, that at the end there were so few surprises left. That by the time she got to Windsor, coming in her search to the last days of her father's life, she had tired of her persona, a young woman with a tape recorder humming carefully beside her, her legs crossed just so, her varnished voice probing the lives of others for the apparent good of society. She began to appear more and more to herself like a Girl Scout leading them smugly into the dangerous territory of a daughter's memory. Like the German's daughter.

She smiles to think that the former students of Wymore College, men almost middle-aged now, might continue to hold reunions, returning with the teachers every so often to the classroom that was once her father's, for the thing they still imagined, perhaps an epiphany. The sensation that it could be any one of them next, slowly going insane. Or else cut down by members of their own families. And then the relief of finding out that their own lives were still intact, that they were still safe from the pain.

That's no doubt why they waited so long that day at the college, guessing what she looked like, whether she would be just about perfect to watch in action, like her father, and just as crazy underneath. They would have willingly made him into a hero, she knows, as much for their own inflated sense of loss and recovery as for her sake.

She has an unpleasant recollection of being stretched taut

by fatigue by the time she arrived at the college, which consisted of a few buildings looking somehow new and uneasy on the landscape, unattached to anything permanent or settled. Like so many other campuses in Canada it looked as though people would learn a sense of isolation and displacement there, and she felt herself to be an intruder from the real world, her clothes hot and pressed to her skin, looking slept-in from the journey, the train two hours late in the Canadian tradition, her breath stale with Scotch from the bar car. Worst of all, she already knew what they would say.

Yes, she knew they would agree that the German had prepared a snotty-nosed bunch of tech-school louts with his magic formula of how to do things right. That the German was always on their backs, always pushing them to do better than even they cared about. They reminded one another of the beginning of the year, when he told them he'd stopped smoking, how proud he'd been of that. Their voices rising in excitement when they remembered how he set up all kinds of standards, not only for their drawing, but for their thinking. For their morals. They admitted then, quietly, how he started smoking again. They murmured then, among outbursts of nervous staccato laughter, how at first they'd been led to believe he'd smashed his Corvair into a concrete abutment on the 401. How it made more sense when they discovered he had killed his wife and neatly, perfectly, finished himself off.

Of course the students insisted that this was somehow part of what he'd been teaching them. That it was a warning. That they grew up in a hurry. That they learned they had to live more carefully, work harder, drink less beer, watch out for the signs, stay out of unnecessary trouble with their friends, their families. They said, in younger voices still hushed by tragedy, that they had wisened up. Oh yeah, in that year life became real for them. In the end they denied they were ever disappointed in the man they called "the German."

"Well, I was disappointed," Else said then, her voice shrill. Shocking them all. Reminding them that the answer was embodied in a thin woman with a raucous laugh who was somehow like the German after all. Leaving them all feeling somehow cheated once again.

A wave of exhaustion sweeps over Else like the warmth of an electric blanket. Yes, she remembers thinking in the middle of the night that if she were to fall asleep she might lose the events and faces of the past few weeks. It was much like her fear of the moon disappearing when she was a child, curled up almost asleep in the back seat of the car, that bright circle of light seeming to follow her home. How afraid she'd been to stop watching, even for a moment, in case her power to draw the moon should somehow dissipate with sleep.

It is not the moon, however, but the sun that is struggling to rise over Toronto, its cold light reaching across the bed stretching empty and flat before her like a featureless horizon. Snow sits heavily on the window ledges and has filled the small holes in the wooden storm windows so that no air can pass in or out of the house. That feels safer somehow to Else. That way there is a definite boundary between the things of the past and the things that follow.

It is only then that Else realizes that Dean has not been home. She can feel she is going to be alone, caught in a shifting pattern of sleep and vigilance peopled only with those she has conjured up from her childhood. The memories she has feared losing all struggling to remain with her, even though they have all finally disappointed her. Every one.

Else remembers walking quietly, almost piously, to the church in Rosetown just a few days ago. The church her father had built. The twenty-foot cross in front of the church, which lit up at night, was rusting where a metal seam between the dark beams had gathered water in other spring thaws. The church smelled damp inside and was full of echoes.

Else was not surprised to see that the pastor had aged; he had seemed only a boy, at least next to her father, when she first knew him as a child. But his boyish naïveté and annoying assurance of things seen behind the curtain — he used to step behind the blood-red drapery before and after the sermons like a magician — that remained. He was wearing black — she imagined he liked his robes of office — and his head was bowed. But there was some pride there yet, in the way his head resisted the downcast expression. And when he walked before her into the rectory, his body was somehow unmoving, solid.

He, like the others, had been saving a small, bittersweet story of her father as though all along he had been expecting her to come and have tea with him in twenty years' time. He seemed sure enough that she had not moved forward from some static place in childhood, as he had not moved from his post in all that time.

He remembered that he had gone out sailing with Else's family. "It was as though he had something to prove," he said solemnly of her father, as though he were connecting the sailing story to the text of a sermon in the future.

They ran aground, the pastor said. And in late November when the lake water was already so cold, the sailing skipper he'd heard so much about had run the boat up on a shelf of rock just outside the breakwaters of his own yacht club. "But it was very foggy," he said, laughing. "Your father couldn't have seen the pastor at the pulpit, I mean at the bowsprit," he said, savouring his own joke.

And the way the pastor told it, it seemed he had offered — a man who couldn't swim had offered — to walk ashore to get help.

But Else knew better; her father had chosen to stay with his beloved boat, it was clear. And had chosen to send the poor young minister, shivering in his underwear and covered in Lanolin, to the shore. She remembered her father's version of the adventure later: "It was a good thing the pastor was well over six feet. The boat drew six feet exactly, so if Pastor Holtz walked in a very straight line and prayed, he could keep his nose above water." Her father's humour had always relied a little on the disadvantage of others.

But despite the cold cream the pastor had caught a chill and at church the next week he was sneezing and sniffling throughout the sermon, the text suspiciously awash with watery images of "souls being lost at sea" or "set adrift on an ocean of disbelief." It was doubtful the usually patient man of God had ever forgiven her father, for when the pastor said goodbye and took Else's hand gently, his eyes seemed to water, as though in deference to that day on the sailboat and his subsequent illness.

In like spirit, Else felt the pastor owed her a debt from childhood, so she said, "Pastor Holtz, do you still believe that dogs cannot enter the Kingdom of Heaven?"

That had been Else's first reason to abandon God, she remembers. Her fight with the Lutheran minister over Thor's death. She was in Sunday school, it was a few weeks after the dog was buried in the spot of high ground next to the wild cherry tree, and Else asked the pastor, who was just then passing through the church basement with his important black robes on, his hands clasped before him, whether the dog would go to heaven. The pastor replied that as animals did not have souls, as they could not make moral choices, they could not therefore enter the Kingdom of Heaven. Else stood up and said with some conviction that her dog had indeed known the difference between right and wrong. Just as she did, and she said calmly that in this case the pastor was wrong.

She was asked to apologize to the pastor, but she would not. And was punished by her father for her wilfulness in church. There was a feeling of satisfaction in this, she remembers, for the dog and she had always been joined by a kind of misunderstanding.

Else supposes now that the dog was brought home as therapy for her on a day when she was still very small — three years old? She was terribly afraid of all the dogs that roamed at large in those days, appearing with seeming premeditation at the butcher's shop, the schoolyard at recess, the streets awaiting garbage trucks. She hated dogs; they seemed to wait for her when she crawled behind her sister beneath the schoolyard fence, sniffing her, their white teeth shining at eye level, their eyes seeming to know of her fear. Once they had followed her home, a whole string of unruly and homeless dogs, following her flight through the basement door and up the dark, steep cellar stairs. She calling breathlessly for help, bursting into the light and warmth of the upstairs hall, her mother there, her arms open. The dogs turning tail and rushing in a pack out the door below, careening down the garden paths, barking madly.

Thus Else's father bought a dog for fifty dollars — a good sum in those days — from the man who owned the gas station near the graveyard. The new puppy, with ears like tents pitched thoughtfully across his head, grew to be a large black dog with only a smudge of rust on his cheeks and across the toes of his big feet; he was handsome, what they called a "police dog" in those days. Looked like he owned the world. But he really owned very little of it. Right from the beginning he was never really wanted in the family.

It was probably that shared feeling of not belonging that drew them together as allies. Else and the dog learned together that it was dangerous to depend too much on the family for affection or any generous or constant display of justice. They used to escape together to the dark space beneath the porch and eat boxes of dog biscuits together. For which she was punished — both for releasing the black dog from his kennel, and for eating what was not hers to eat — as if to prove her theory that the dog was fast becoming her best friend. Else can still taste the mealy biscuits, wet with the dog's saliva as he tried to savour each one that went her way as well as his; the green ones shaped like bones were her favourites.

Thor — named after the fierce Norse god of thunder — was rarely allowed in the house except when his fear of thunderstorms became too piteous a thing to be heard. Then he was sometimes allowed in to slink beneath the kitchen table until the storm passed. At least until the day he upended the table, set with bowls of her mother's thick pea soup, and then ran full tilt into the living room, where her father's drawings for some church were spread on the floor. Crouched there in his fright, he peed on the paper smelling of ammonia, while the thunder crashed overhead. He was dragged from the house, a huge black dog hanging limp from her father's hands and bleating strangely, and was left to spend the evening outside with the fading lightning and thunder. But after her father's terrible anger, the storm must have seemed a relief. Else came out after dinner and sat on the steps freshly washed from the rain, feeding the defeated black dog his dinner, spoonful by spoonful, out of a can of Dr. Ballard's she had opened herself. Their friendship grew out of mishap and their shared fears of living up to her father's expectations.

That is the thing about memory, Else thinks, as the severe light of a winter's day passes into the room and makes her draw the blanket closer to her, as though bringing a kind of cold, not warmth. The things she remembers fondly of the dog no one else in the family ever seemed to see. The fact that he used to pick Else up from kindergarten, six blocks away, never minding the distraction of the roaming dogs who wanted to play or fight, never deviating from his duty, bringing her safely home day in and day out, was simply expected from a dog alleged by her father to be a smart dog. No one had taught him this; he simply did it. And for little reward beside Else's kind tugs of his ears or gay tumbles with him in the grassy ditches along the way home.

The stories her father told of the dog were always unkind; they seemed to focus on the day he'd gone with Else to a Field-Day parade with the red fire engines in it, and the bicycles of every kid she knew dressed up with crêpe paper in the spokes. She had gone as Little Red Riding Hood with Thor as the wolf. The dog had started to strain a little on the leash when the sirens from the fire engines began to whine, and in his confusion started snapping at children dressed as pirates and clowns. Else's father, disappointed as usual, took Else and the dog home even though the school principal wanted to give the fairy tale pair first prize. Else ran all the way back to the school then, crying, thinking only of the plaque that would have her name and Thor's engraved on it. But the prize had already been awarded to one of those bicycles.

And her father chose to forget the time Thor had protected them, her sister and herself, while out playing in the wild fields behind the house. A stray, a large, lean buff-coloured dog, had run after the girls while they were playing, and Thor appeared and brought the dog to the ground, mauling the stray so badly he limped around the neighbourhood with a shorter leg for years afterward, making a large circle around Else's house and the fields behind. Her sister had been bitten trying to get the struggling dogs apart, and for that, once again, Thor was blamed.

The field behind the house was the place Thor was buried the day he attacked Else's father. It was the sickness he had that made him do it, Else was told then. Although now she wonders if it was not simply something he had been biding his time about. Waiting. He was sick, though, she remembers. He had streams of thick green discharge running from his eyes and nose, had stopped eating, and seemed to be preoccupied with licking his paws and looking far off into the distance. Else would comfort him, giving him sacks to lie on and ice cubes to lick, but he shivered so that his teeth rattled and he seemed to forget who she was.

And one day, when her father went to feed him — he was tied to a white birch behind the house — he leaped at her father with a strange gargling noise in his throat. It was just growing dark, her mother and father talked quietly, and Else was asked to set the table for supper. She remembers putting the glasses and plates down carefully in the brightly lit dining room, and not being able to see past the black panes of glass.

But she could almost sense when her father raised the gun to shoot the dog; Thor broke the rope and ran wildly about, seeming to look for cover, running into tree trunks in the swamp. The mud sucking him down, he was so weak, the mud making him an easy victim with her father's first shot. Yes, there was only one shot while Else was setting the table that night. And her mother's voice explaining that the dog had gone blind and was vicious because of the distemper. That there was nothing else to do.

Else remembers staring at the pastor and waiting for his answer — she understood moral choices so much better now.

"You told me once that you could see their souls in their eyes," he said, blinking furiously. "And since I'm so busy with the souls of my sheep —" he smiled weakly, congratulating himself for his maneuvre through an uncomfortable moment — "and I've never had a dog, I'll have to take your word for it."

"Thank you," she said, as in those days when the congregation filtered out and shook the pastor's hand, blinking in the sunshine by the front doors. And as in those days, she felt empty and entirely alone.

She remembers the dull pain of looking up Henry Schneer, the contractor, the next day. The man with metallic blue eyes set incongruously in a rather placid coarse face. A face that could be brutal. She had never known him well as a child; he was one of her father's friends who rarely spoke to the children. Simply passed them. Wearing clothes with cement on the cuffs or a smear of paint on his massive shirt fronts. She thought he looked exactly the same now, except richer. When Else arrived at a house with ornate porticos and fountains, designed to deny his hard-working past, he came to the door wearing an expensive cardigan with a blood-red wound of paint on the left sleeve.

And right away he told Else that her father had planned the shooting beforehand. As though she might not have known that, and as though it was, if not bad news, the kind that might make a daughter blush, then merely information. "Well, of course I didn't know that then," he added, as though he might be an accomplice in a bad made-for-TV drama. "But he asked to borrow the Walther .38 from my collection of handguns some weeks before the affair. For target practice with some of his teaching friends," he said.

Of course Henry had said no, never intuiting anything beyond the alleged gun practice then. He said to her father that he could get into a lot of trouble with the law if there were some kind of accident.

"I know you're probably a good shot," I said to him. "Boy, what a laugh! You know he was a strange guy, your father. When everything in his life was peachy keen, he complained bitterly of not having enough. Enough money, enough time to play on his boat, enough recognition for his designs. But that day, when he came to borrow the gun, he said that everything in his life was perfect. That you kids and Charlotte were excited about his new job in Windsor, that he was building a new house on an old dance pavilion. And then the bugger starts to dance, actually dance in my office."

"What kind of dance?" Else asked.

"Oh, you couldn't give that kind of dance a name. It wasn't a tango or a fox trot." Schneer laughed and put an arm around her shoulder and squeezed her hard. "So you come and see me again, O.K.? Don't lose touch." That was it , no questions about her life. He, like the pastor, had saved something to say about his friend, Gerhard, and it had been said.

It was not until her meeting with Heffler that she fell apart. She is only glad now that she had the sense to leave his office before he had time to capitalize on a young woman coming apart at the seams. Or he would have offered her long-term therapy, or at least a drink in a small, covert bar somewhere, making certain she was somehow in his debt for the feelings he had aroused in her.

She remembers how he grew steadily more chatty and confidential, as though they were finally conspirators in the truth that he found his job boring, that he thought very little of people with problems. He called himself a family counsellor, but the truth was that he despised the dynamics of loving when they broke down. She suspected he even despised women in the way that men do who build pedestals to create harder falls. She remembers having the sensation that he was leading up to asking her out for dinner and then a quick one-night stand, letting his wife know that he was working late. He probably had a gadget on his phone that allowed him to make those kinds of plans with a light touch of his finger.

When he first gave her his hand in greeting she thought she detected a hint of man touching woman. A faint suggestion of flirtation, or at the least, flattery. And there was a hint of barter, more than compromise, in his partronizing smile. "I don't make a habit of talking to journalists or students about my profession," he said, although he seemed eager to talk about himself to the daughter of a former patient, now dead. He swayed back and forth lazily in his swivel chair, entertaining her as though on his yacht at the R.C.Y.C., showing her the trinkets on his desk, telling her pleasant anecdotes about his schooling in Europe. He was a man who had apparently not aged enough in fifteen years; his abundant jet black hair had only the slightest streaks of grey at the temples. With his oversize jacket made even more flamboyant by wide, pastel stripes, his Gatsby-like white tassled loafers, his eyes narrowed to a deliberate squint that would deflect any insight into his character, he looked like a shady character out of an old movie, a swaggering gangster from the twenties. And like a gangster he seemed to be saying he was in top form, a snappy dresser, still in control. That there was no messing with Heffler.

Else didn't waste any time getting him onto the subject of dangerousness. How did a psychiatrist measure that in an individual, she asked, the capability of taking a life, not simply imagining it. As she spoke she imagined taking a small handgun from her purse, perhaps the very one Schneer had refused her father, and blowing the art deco lamp off the wall behind Heffler, the frosted glass falling in a shower over his startled face. Just to give him the sensation. Just to make him take her seriously.

"We are here to reflect some of the possibilities, perhaps. But we do not take responsibility for our patients' actions. How could we? That would be more religion than medicine," he said. Laughing then, his laughing ending in the same way as all of his phrasing, with a nasty, hissing sound that made her think of a missile hitting a target. That seemed to say he was used to being the more successful in so many conversations.

She suddenly longed to remind the doctor that she was not so different from the stiff-faced girl of sixteen who had once imagined his downcast eyes to be a sign of his guilt, not merely evasion. She still had an impression of his narrow eyes, inscrutable, looking down, that day of the inquest. Heffler mumbling so that the court reporter had to repeatedly ask him to speak up. So that even "the children of the deceased," as they were known, had to strain to hear the terrible things that were being said. Else remembered Heffler's voice drawn into himself as though for protection, the annoying repetition of the phrase, "we had no choice but to . . . ," and how he passed the sorry subject of her father's actions to his colleagues in a smooth language of absolution only they could understand, words like "follow-up" and "family contact" floating around the room like bubbles bursting over the heads of the listeners.

Of course there had been follow-up of a kind. Although Heffler had stated at the inquest that Mrs. Rainer had not co-operated with the doctors, he had phoned once to see why Mr. Rainer hadn't been attending his outpatient treatments. And to check whether he was still taking his medication, the small yellow pills he'd prescribed to render him sluggish and less sensitive, as it were, to his own life. When Else's mother had whispered hoarsely, "He's not here," the doctor hadn't been eager enough to discover why she refused to talk about her husband. Of course how was he to guess that the man he'd treated with shock treatments and anti-depressants, who'd been sent home "greatly improved," was standing beside her, mouthing obscenities and making threats. That was summer, a full eight or nine months after his brief stay in hospital; Else remembered how her father had tried to strangle her mother that day with the telephone cord.

But she could see how Heffler was a man prone to forgetting the stark and accusing look of a teenage girl who'd had to take the stand that day and describe the effects of pyschiatric assessment on a family of five. Even then it had seemed to have more to do with religion; the bodies had been disposed of, after all, in a narrow grave which held them both, keeping them unwillingly together, even after death. When you're sixteen and you are asked to pronounce your own parents' times of death, comparatively that is, and you cock your head strangely as if listening again to their side-by-side seesaw breathing . . . . When you've been repeatedly asked who died first, the one with the neat head wound joining words to action in a final, no-nonsense way, or the one with the numerous wounds in the throat, shoulders, chest, wearing them like blood-red medals in the war between men and women, and you catch the look of surprise on all the faces when you finally declare it was the latter that rattled on, lips moving in some extended faith, who in fact died a messy second . . . to a sixteen-year-old surely that was a case of religion, not medicine.

But fifteen years later she could see more clearly that Heffler had never had any feelings of responsibility about her parents' deaths. She could feel the difference between them — how he had gone on, and how she had never stopped thinking about all the things that could have been done. How his velvety soft retreat from that small courtroom north of Toronto years ago had led him directly to the plush office building he now presided over in much the same way he'd once been superintendant of Shoreline. True, he was closer to his patients here than he'd been as a younger man in the decrepit, fortress-like hospital, but somehow farther from the truth of their stale and desperate lives. Here he sold a kind of insulation to the past; here the feet moved softly on the thick carpets, the glass was tinted to allow only a comfortable brightness in the cool, clean rooms, and the plants bowed benignly to the troubled visitors. Henry Mancini and Bing Crosby tunes played placidly in the waiting room and there were bright murals on the walls, giant abstract shapes in primary colours designed to daunt a patient into childish hopefulness. Here anger and disappointment over the past were intended to seem unreasonable.

Of course that's the way it had all been left the day of the inquest. When it was over, the cops, the pathologist, the shrinks, even the coroner, left the room in hushed voices, looking at the three children in the front row with some antipathy, as though the vague conclusions reached that day about the nature of tragedy might follow them home to their supper tables. Even then she could see that everyone just wanted to forget and that she would have the larger and larger questions inside her until something else happened. She felt, even then, that there was a danger in them all leaving the inquest so uncertain as to who was to blame.

She practically scared the pants off the fellow who'd been the court reporter at the time, when she tracked him down to a Nissan dealership a few weeks ago. He'd become a car salesman, and recognized her right away, balking only for a moment before selling her a copy of the proceedings for fifty bucks. "These are dead files anyway," he said, never appreciating the irony in the comment. "So I don't suppose it matters if you have them." But the whole time he couldn't take his eyes off of her, the way she had just materialized fifteen years later. He followed her out to the parking lot, and leaned on the bright bronze fender of a pick-up. "Just off the boat," he said, although he stopped short of suggesting she trade up from her old station wagon. Somehow he knew she wasn't in the mood.

When she read the hefty report she suddenly remembered the five startled faces, three men and two women, who'd been subpoenaed for jury duty. A stone mason, a salesclerk at Eaton's, a house painter, housewife, and one unemployed; their job to sit back and listen, and in their own awkward and uncomprehending ways, to pass judgment. The five found that her father was "mentally *dranged* at intervals for *quiet* some time." Their poor spelling and uncertain concept of time didn't make Else confident that anything had been gained that day. The five also wrote, albeit reluctantly, a recommendation to be entered into the coroner's files. She knew the damn thing off by heart: "To prevent *past* tragedies of this nature we recommend follow-up on *patience* by a *confident* investigator."

Fifteen years later Else seemed to have inherited the full weight of the recommendation; she found herself doing follow-up on a dead man, with great patience. She was the "confident investigator." It was once again a day in April and she was watching the tassles swinging on those bright loafers, Heffler leaning back in his chair and tapping his feet, as though he were at a dance and hearing a lively tune. She couldn't help thinking that it all came back to the shoes.

She remembered asking her brother on the day of the inquest whether he'd noticed their shoes, the doctors' shoes. But Martin had only looked sullen, like he might slug her. So she supposed she was the only one that had been aware of it, the way the several doctors from Shoreline asked to testify wore almost identical pairs of tight, pointed Oxfords, gleaming a freshly polished black the morning of the inquest. Shoes that gave nothing away, simply carried the doctors away very quietly to safety at the end of the day, a cautious chorus line of men above reproach. Somehow she'd given herself reason to believe that the doctors might be wearing sandals on a slushy day of Ontario spring weather. Sandals — watermarked and swollen with winter socks — that would have given her hope. Hope that they might have shared some common ground with her father. He had been well known for wearing socks and sandals year-round.

It was always a surprise, after hearing her father's sharp words and following his equally sharp outline down the impeccably pressed pant of his pale grey suits, to find sandals there. It was a kind of relief for the person meeting him a first time, or even for his long-time friends, she was sure, to see the toes out there in front of him, gripping the floor, wriggling like a child's in anticipation, or curling in dismay. Pointing stiffly with suspicion. After seeing his sandals people often knew what to expect.

But Heffler and the others hadn't taken any special note of the kind of man who hadn't changed his shoes when he changed his continents, when the times demanded change. A man who was desperately vulnerable in a world of tight, pointed shoes imitating the cowboy boot, the kind of shoe that cramps men, driving their feet numb all the way out to their suburban pastures. He was the kind to slip on heavy, black galoshes over the inveterate socks and sandals on a slushy winter day in Toronto. An almost comical gesture, and the sandals, it was true, seemed to make him appear almost affable. But they were also a warning. These were the shoes of a man who lived a great deal in dreams of sailing around the world, and had already built the boat to prove it. Anyone with any sense believed in her father because of his sandals, and soon grew aware of the danger in that belief.

That's what she wanted to explain to Heffler so that he would finally understand. She longed to tell him how the sandals had been a dead give-away, how they had described a man whose survival was measured by enormous risk, a man who had no proper sense of recovery from failure. She wanted to hear Heffler talk about that. She wanted to finally make him accountable for a scene in the past in which he'd counselled her father on the faith required in continuing to live.

Of course she knew she was getting anxious; she could feel her heart visibly pounding behind her V-neck sweater. The office felt suddenly overheated and unbearably binding. Heffler's voice seemed to be repeating over and over again, too quickly, too easily, like some sort of menacing school yard chant, "mother, father, violence, death."

"Of course it's very rare. Otherwise we in the profession wouldn't sleep too well at night," he said, smiling at the suggestion of his own safety being threatened. And she imagined once more reaching for that small gun and pointing it at Heffler, to undermine his confidence once and for all. Had she had the gun, had she pressed the trigger, even then she knew she would undoubtedly have missed, distracted by the sleek, white slip-on shoes, her head bowed down with the tears that were suddenly stinging like nettles on all the soft surfaces of memory.

He must have felt the anger blossom in her and fall short of its mark, perhaps seen her shoulders shake a little. Perhaps she sniffed. For he gathered up his years of training and homed in on her with frightening accuracy, his cool eyes appraising. "You've got a boyfriend, don't you, Else? A steady one, I mean. A man you might one day marry? What's he doing letting a good-looking chick like you run around the countryside putting shrinks on the stand?"

She realized then he'd been deliberately mocking her all along. There was suddenly a feeling in her of something caught halfway between despair and desperate laughter, rising in waves inside her chest, coming out finally like an attack of whooping cough. The sound coming out of her again and again, making it plainer and plainer to her that she didn't have a husband, that she might never marry if she were to measure a man by the improbable standards of her father's shoes.

She rose from her chair then, and walked stiffly from the room, holding her side as though the grieving laughter might escape. She had forgotten to turn off the tape recorder in her handbag; later she could hear the way her high heels tittered all the way down the hall. The sound growing faster and faster as though she were finally running back to her car.

Else hasn't been able to bring herself to listen to the tape again until now. She pulls the tape recorder dispiritedly from her overnight bag and slips in the cassette. She still can't believe Heffler had once counselled her parents.

> I know your father thought I was a scavenger on human misery. He said so and I told him, "You have the charm of a Prussian officer." And it turned out we were both partly right. Oh, yes, I called his bluff. He liked to challenge people and I would size him up and give him my return challenge. I thought, that's the only thing this guy's going to respect.
>
> So I remember laughing with him a bit the first time — your father came twice. That was a compliment to me, I thought; he wasn't the type to roll over and play dead and go see a psychiatrist. It was actually our different experiences of the army, of the war, that got us talking. We sparred a little bit, and I ended up saying to him, "You know, you are an anachronism. They don't make people like you anymore. You are so opinionated, so authoritarian, that it's almost a joke."

So Else has not merely dreamed the damage Heffler might have done, using his confidence as a weapon. Like a man moving with a scythe through others' lives.

> And yet when he came the second time, with your mother, he did not laugh. The sixties was a scene of a terrific power struggle where women were moving out of the roles they had previously accepted and your parents — you could see it — were engaged in a desperate struggle. And your father was very much the "wounded lion." His very sensitive ego was his downfall. All this coming-on-strong business was covering up for a terrible sense of inferiority. I could see

> that when they were both together. And although he would never admit it, I could see that he felt within the marriage — I don't think it was the same with his career, or other things — but with your mother, he felt himself to be a failure.

So far, so good, Else thinks. He should restrict his practice to sparring with wounded lions.

> Your mother was also an anachronism, I suppose. She was the long-suffering type, who has a strange kind of strength. For a long time she was absorbed into this kind of lukewarm existence of not making decisions, not carrying too great a responsibility — you'll have to excuse me here — it's like warm pee, it has certain comforts. For a long time she couldn't get the strength she needed to get out of the situation because she was using so much strength just existing —

There is some static then, and the sound of someone exhaling several times. He smoked a lot, and Else can hear him puffing like crazy. Maybe he was nervous about saying the next part.

> And then she got a whiff of freedom, of liberation, and the more she was pushing for it, the more she was putting your father on the defensive, the more he was coming back at her. All that violence . . . all I could see for them to do was go their separate ways. So . . . I strongly suggested separation at the time.

The tape runs on silently for several minutes, as though Else is hoping for something more.

Obviously Heffler was the one Dr. Gifford had been so upset with years before. "We came to a bad pass over the subject of your father," Dr. Gifford said rather quietly the other day. "I called Heffler some names better left unsaid, and he offered me psychiatric help. We behaved like children," he admitted.

Of course Dr. Gifford would always have a special place with Else because she will always remember his voice sounding like a rescue from a long, unrelenting childhood that day she crawled across the frost-ridden roof to the neighbour's and called him to come and pick her father up. Doctors still made house calls then, Else thinks.

She remembers his visits to her bedside on those stale days of sickness as a child. He was habitually in a hurry and would pull out one of those old pocket watches you'd hope your family doctor would have and then pause, looking off in the distance as though he had a choice to make, not just a series of appointments with people stifled by old age or disease in their darkened houses. He would then place his watch back into the vest pocket of his antiseptic-smelling tweed jacket and set his jaw firmly, prescribing intangible things to go along with his small brown-glassed bottles of medicine. Stories are important, he'd say, preferably in cloth-covered books handed down from older members of the family. Or he would give advice about how she could count the bars of sunlight spread upon her bed or see patterns in the otherwise random flowers on her torn wallpaper.

Once he'd spent an entire evening at their house talking to her father of sailing while her mother had tiptoed in and out of the room smelling of hot mustard plasters, her arms carrying flannel sheets hot from the oven. Her father's eyes had wavered uncertainly over some distant horizon framing his pneumonia and Dr. Gifford had remained there, by the bed, laughing and reliving some of Gerhard's tall tales of his children in the makeshift crow's nest, the storm over the sand bars in Youngstown, the year they won the Susan Hood race by a halyard.

Else remembers the thing she used to call the doctor as a child. His orange handlebar moustache had always reminded her of the toilet brush her mother kept tucked behind the bathroom door. So she shamelessly called him Dr. Toilet Brush; it became a term of endearment she carried into her teens, when she teetered on the arms of the old chair in his office, plucking the brass tacks from the seat back, her mother's face pale against the maroon leather.

He was not the man she remembered from those days, however, when she paid him a surprise visit last week. No, this Dr. Gifford had become weary. She could see that right away. She could feel his age; the years had thinned his red moustache and she found he was frowning, if not at her, then at life. Directly at life. When the light from the lamp overhead shone in his face, he pushed it aside. He seemed impatient. And he stretched the edges of his heavy tweed jacket over his stomach — when he noticed Else watching him, he said, "My wife hates this. Now the jacket will hang lower in front unless buttoned."

That was not the kind of detail that had troubled him fifteen years earlier. For a few minutes he and Else sat, saying nothing. Listening to Mrs. Stremple packing up in the waiting room. The radio was switched off, the filing cabinet closed uneasily once more. The patients had all gone home and snow was falling in the streets outside. Everything seemed to be waiting. Even Mrs. Stremple. "You can go, Mrs. Stremple," the doctor said wearily. And she moved away from his door then to the outside entrance. They heard her slide on her small black overboots and she was gone.

Even then the doctor seemed loathe to talk. The doctor who had once always had time to talk to his patients; the waiting rooms had been overflowing with the mildly sick and measled and he'd talked to them endlessly of their hopes and desires, their heartaches and lack of sleep. He'd habitually been hours behind in his appointments, but his patients, connected together like one unhappy family, had never seemed to mind waiting their turns.

Else remembered him taking every slim opportunity to talk

with her as a child. And then, after her parents . . . did he remember? She'd been in a lilac bathing suit, sitting on a split rail fence amid the fields ablaze in the heat of August. Sixteen, sitting among the ragweed and the golden rod, her parents dead not quite a year, she was sniffing with the allergies she'd developed as a kind of final homage to them — and there Dr. Gifford had suddenly appeared. His car crunched into view on that old gravel road that ran down to the river and was used only by lovers on summer nights. And she said with a sneeze, and some disdain, that she was fine. Just fine. He shouldn't have troubled looking for her, no matter what Lily might have told him. She was clearly angry at the invasion of even this, her private moments in a field somewhere in summer.

Yes, in the past few weeks, she'd once again felt the threat of their invasiveness, the doctors. Too early, too late.

"I used to get such earaches, remember?" Else asked suddenly. Connecting him unwillingly, oh so unwillingly, to her past.

Dr. Gifford adjusted his jacket once again, as though agitated by some change in the dark hound's-tooth jacket he'd worn for so many years. "When there was trouble at home, your brother and sister had the good sense to grow stronger, so they could leave home further behind. But not you, Else. You had coughs and colds and earaches and tonsils infected, so you could remain at home, close to the fighting. You wanted to sacrifice yourself for your parents piece by piece. So finally, when you had the stomach aches — you didn't know I put you in hospital to protect you, did you? — I had your appendix cut out. Even that to save you from yourself.

"And your father came to the hospital in the middle of the night and carried you off. There was that big fiasco about the nurse who had flicked her cigarette ash into the glass holding your thermometer. So your father cursed the nurses and shouted in your ear that home was much better for healing.

Carried your newly bandaged twelve-year-old body — you were heavily medicated and fast asleep, thin as a stick — back to the scene of your greatest suffering, just so he could be the hero he was constantly failing to be. To prove his love, I suppose."

Else suddenly remembered how Dr. Gifford had shown her the appendix in a small jar. As if to show her the pain had been removed and give her proof. She had looked bravely at it, then at him. "You asked to see it, remember?" he'd said with his British chin-up smartness. "I asked what it looked like," she'd admitted weakly.

"In spite of the apparent frailty of your health," Dr. Gifford said suddenly, looking at Else directly with some of the old sparkle yet in his eyes, "you were always the tough one, weren't you?"

Else supposed that was a compliment from a man who had told her once that he'd had only four hours of sleep a night to get through medical school while working nights in a grocery store.

"The first inkling I had of something seriously wrong in your family was when your mother told me about that sailing trip to the Thousand Islands. It was autumn, school had already started, and you had just come back from vacation. I ran into your mother on the street." The doctor glanced at Else then, sitting in that chair where her mother had looked so burdened years before, and some resemblance between the two women seemed to startle him. "And although she'd spent months on the water, in the sun, she looked pale and thin, with what seemed to me a worried look. She seemed preoccupied with something. She tried to laugh, I remember, when she spoke of the family's many episodes; the whirlpools, the seaweed round the engine propeller and your father diving beneath the hull like Tarzan, with a knife in his mouth. But then she gradually became more serious, saying how your father liked to sail into harbours under full sail, using his own children's arms and legs as bumpers against the docks 'so his damn boat wouldn't get scratched,' was I think how she put it. And that was the first time I remember your mother sounding angry about anything."

Dr. Gifford narrowed his eyes, as though looking hard at some point about to disappear into the past. "And then she told me how your father had sailed in full spinnaker down the Murray Canal, barely two boat lengths wide, with you at the tiller. You at twelve, thirteen? — blowing the foghorn, the swing bridges barely having time to open before the boat went through at full tilt, a strong westerly wind behind you. That's when your mother started crying, right here on Maple Street — when I asked her why you were at the helm.

"That's when she told me your father was holding her prisoner in the cabin, beating her and calling her names. And meanwhile you maneuvred the boat down the Murray Canal, single-handedly."

Dr. Gifford seemed to be looking up at the bumblebee-striped spinnaker billowing out before the boat, drawing the family of five to some sort of tragic destination. "I've always thought it was the way you suffered on that trip that made your mother confide in someone. And it was right then, while she wiped away her tears quickly and seemed ashamed she'd mentioned anything, that I called the psychiatrists at the hospital. And it was their opinion, on that day of autumn, that the situation was dangerous.

"Of course, I felt the danger." Dr. Gifford shifted in his seat, as though bracing himself. "Your father drew into himself, keeping his family apart from friends or visitors. I recall feeling I wasn't welcome at your house that autumn — I missed that German coffee cake your mother used to make — so I asked your father to come in and see me. I knew I couldn't tell him what your mother had said to me. I knew that. I had to somehow establish myself as being the only one who knew he had problems. But putting myself in that position, where he might feel I was the only one outside the family that knew of his trouble — well, let's just say I had the good sense to meet him in my office with a policeman standing by outside. Behind the forsythia by the window.

"You see, I knew what would bother your father. In those days the family was still a hard nut to crack. You couldn't get in, and you couldn't get out. If there was tragedy there, inside the tough shell, it was not something you shared.

"And there was the concept of shame, of course, shame that the family was not holding up as well as it ought to be. The head of the family, your father, took that shame upon himself.

"Anyway, he came in, impeccably dressed, the usual well-mannered, intelligent individual. I didn't push any points until he had vented his feelings and then I tried suggesting he seek help, and there was some emotion welled up inside and he didn't actually cry, but his voice cracked. . . . However, there was no hope of him consenting to any treatment.

"I held off doing anything. But the situation came to a head again; your mother phoned my wife and said she was having a dreadful time, that Gerhard was treating her roughly, that he had threatened to shoot her. I couldn't understand why she hadn't removed the gun — but she said she was too frightened to touch it. She said that he wouldn't let her out of his sight, that she was almost a prisoner. She told me she couldn't stand it anymore, that she'd be willing to let her name be used as the source of information for committal.

"My great fear at this stage was that once I acted, I knew I would never have another chance to step inside the house. Because your father was a man of honour, you see, and he would interpret this as a breach of trust."

The doctor sat hunched forward, as though on a journey, anticipating some sudden stop. He was red in the face, whether from the heat of his tweed jacket or from some inner pressure, Else couldn't say. But she thought once again that he looked tired. He was tired of the waiting, the readiness, and never being on time. The doctor was plainly tired.

"I was wrong." He said those words painfully and waited until the snowplow outside had passed, its grating noise causing him to close his eyes and sigh. "And then perhaps because I was wrong, I failed to recognize them that night. I never did see your mother and father again until that night in December, when she lay in the snow, and it was all over. A man and a woman were lying on the road, looking for all the world in that darkness as though they were making snow angels. How could I have failed to know that it was your parents, finally and terribly dead on the roadside, when I'd been expecting something like that for so long?"

The doctor bowed his head, was fingering his moustache with shaking fingers. Else remembered how she'd hated him giving injections because his hands always shook.

"When I think of it now — my God, I looked for a pulse in your mother's wrist. The police were counting the holes the bullets had made passing into the snowbanks and shaking their heads, and I was the new coroner, kneeling in the road —"

The phone rang loudly in the small office, making Else startle. The doctor said something about potatoes and mint sauce; it was his wife calling. He put down the phone receiver carefully.

"I didn't know until I had supper set before me hours later and the commissioner called. I remember asking the commissioner to repeat the names: Rainer, Rainer. And that's when I learned you had seen the whole thing. I always felt badly that I hadn't stayed to comfort you at the Littler's, where you'd gone for help."

"You shouldn't blame yourself," Else said then, somewhat impatiently. This was not where she'd intended to lay blame. Not with Dr. Gifford.

But when she saw his eyes glistening, she found it easy to forgive the man with the fox-coloured moustache who had led her father away in his pajamas one Sunday morning toward all the other doctors. She knew that Dr. Gifford had probably aged on that morning more than any other. That there were probably the first signs of salt strewn in his red moustache after that day.

As she was leaving she leaned toward him and gave him a slight kiss on the cheek, which embarrassed him.

"You know what the commissioner told me that night?" he continued, worrying the subject. Trying to get something pithy out of the scene, even after all the years. "He told me you were silent, defiant, the day your parents died. That you were angry with what the others, those outside the family, had seen that night. That you never cried at all."

Else remembers that she hadn't cried even at the funeral. She draws one of Dean's sweaters closer around herself and thinks back to the funeral. The funeral with the closed caskets; the students from the college had sent flowers with no message, simply their names. Henry Schneer, Dr. Gifford, and Uncle had been among the pallbearers, and there were a few other men from the congregation. Else remembers thinking during the service that it required a great many friends to carry a dead man, that a dead man was somehow heavier than the sum of his life. She and her brother, Martin, had once lifted their father off the ground for a moment by laughingly grabbing him around the thighs. Professing their strength after that day.

The funeral required a different kind of lifting. The pastor had asked a great deal of God that day, Else remembers. And although the mouths of those paying their respects — it had been a small service — had been pressed tight, almost painfully closed, holding back the stories, Uncle had bravely stood up and said a few words.

Uncle had called him an Elizabethan, she remembers. A man who could do everything well, who had an interest in the universe. A gentleman, the brightest man he'd ever met. A man who left one with a sense of urgency and energy to do the things one was capable of doing.

Else thinks of her father's best friend now. A man attached

to an oxygen machine who has to take deep breaths these days in order to speak kindly of his friends. And in the aging process something once intact, once understood, has loosened. Is no longer understood. It was on a Sunday, like the Sundays of her childhood, that they sat together at either end of the paisley couch, to better balance the history between them. Sipping Uncle's best single malt, they had seemed like conspirators in the fact that they had both long romanticized her father.

He had started once again at the beginning, explaining the summer they met, her father searching in his broken language for a place to settle with his family. Uncle, gardening, taking them in on that heavy summer's day. And thirty years later, only days before his death, her father once again seeking out the street on which Uncle still lives, where Uncle is still outside, still bending over the earth. But this time it is late autumn. Her father is still searching for the right words in English for something he imagines. He tells Uncle that Charlotte has left him, has taken the children. Just like that. Right out of the blue. And just as in that moment years before, Uncle remains calm, continues raking leaves. Hands his friend Gerhard a rake.

It is no longer land Gerhard wants, he can see that. This time it is love.

"Your father offered to take us out for dinner then," Uncle said. "To a posh restaurant; he obviously needed our company badly. I protested a little, mainly on Lily's behalf, because she hadn't been feeling up to snuff lately. Feeling faint and lacking appetite.

"But your father talked us into it, and we were surprised to see Charlotte there as well. She was wearing a yellow dress that your father had always liked, but there were dark circles under her eyes and she looked more wistful than usual. And didn't seem as patient as she'd always been with Gerhard when he started boasting of his new job at the college, and how his family was going to move out and join him soon. The kids were really looking forward to it, he said. Your mother looked away then, and quickly left the table for the washroom.

"When Lily followed her a little later because of an upset stomach, your mother told her everything of the months prior to the separation. How Gerhard had been tapping the phone, how he was following her to school, even yet.

"We went back to your house then, even though Lily said she wasn't feeling at all well. Of course your mother hadn't seen the house in some weeks, since the separation. It was your father's idea to go there; perhaps he was looking for a way to make Charlotte vulnerable, to make her sorry.

"There was a horrible scene then, in which your father started accusing your mother of ruining his career, of breaking up his family. He became so worked up that I had to separate the two of them. That's how I became an unwilling arbitrator between husband and wife, carrying messages back and forth down the long hallway between the rooms that kept them apart.

"Charlotte stayed in the living room, holding Lilian's hand where she lay on the couch. Poor Lily had to lie down suddenly, overcome by dizziness and nausea. Of course we all thought it was the uproar making her feel faint, but that was the beginning of the Parkinson's, I suppose."

Uncle turned on the oxygen machine then, took a few deep breaths, and continued. He'd lost his best friend and his wife in the space of a few years, and his own grip on events, once certain, was slipping.

"So I stayed with your father in his study, and there would be some discussion, if you could call it that — and then I would convey your father's unbending replies to your mother's wishes.

"It was odd; for once your mother was asking something of your father, and was not backing down. There were two things she wanted: to finish teaching that year, so her teaching certificate would be secure, and a sum of money for her own.

"Your father, of course, didn't agree with that at all; he

could see the money represented her freedom from him. 'Never!' he shouted. 'I will never give her that!' And the look in his eyes was that of a madman.

"I understood then why your mother was afraid. Before that moment I had never really believed her fear, when she said he had threatened her and the children. Why, I thought to myself, he loves his family so much, he's a little stubborn perhaps, old-worldly, prosaic. But he's a reasonable man.

"And then I asked him, 'Do you really love Charlotte? I think she's asking whether you love her.' "

Else could imagine Uncle's quiet deliberate voice asking the question and her father answering, "Yes, I do," sobered by his renewal of old vows in a dark and empty house before his oldest witness.

But the worst was when Uncle had gone with the message back to her mother and had asked her the same thing. "How about you, Charlotte, do you love Gerhard?" She said nothing. Uncle said her eyes were puffy from crying, and that she twisted the wedding ring on her left hand, and said nothing.

Uncle was naturally shocked by her reaction, just as he was shocked when it came out that evening that Gerhard had once accused her of having an affair with Uncle. When Uncle told Else that, there on the paisley couch, she felt as though he had admitted her into the cruel privileges of adulthood. "You understand, despite the fact that I admired your mother immensely, how ridiculous that accusation was," he said, scoffing somewhat at the idea of it.

Else looked at him, still a handsome man in his seventies, still wearing the cravats he was famous for. It may have been ridiculous to imagine her mother placing love elsewhere, but it was not too hard to imagine that she deserved some love in her direction. And that other men, even friends, had imagined the things she deserved.

Else was only thirteen when she learned the consequences of being faithful, when she'd gone with her mother one day to the "group conference," as they'd called it. Her father was in the hospital then, for thirty days observation, for his "dangerous" behaviour. Her mother had warned her that she wasn't to say anything. Then why was she going? "It may help to have you there. It may help your father," was all she said. When Else thinks of it now, she thinks it may have helped if she hadn't been there. To have let her father rant and rave and carry on.

But they tried to carry off these conversations with some dignity; there was coffee served, the chairs were all pulled quietly into some shape resembling a circle, and then the words would begin.

"Please sit down, Mrs. Rainer."

"Yes, thank you. Thank you." Her mother had an annoying habit of saying things like that twice. To make sure she was pleasing everyone.

Her father was eyeing her with cold, stiff eyes, and the shrink was shuffling pages in a file folder as though waiting. It seemed her mother already had tear-brimmed eyes, and she looked nervously from one man to the other, from her husband to the doctor. From the doctor to her husband.

Else's father, lean from his days in hospital, looked with his hard eyes at her mother, scraped his chair closer to hers and said, "Let's get going, doctor. I'm sure my wife will agree."

"That's an interesting comment, Mr. Rainer," said the doctor, who was sitting like the apex of the triangle across from the couple loosely linked by their apprehension. "Let's begin there."

"What do you mean?" her father said, suddenly smiling, suddenly harshly charming. Realizing his mistake with the doctor.

"Why do you speak for your wife, do you think? Do you do that a lot?"

Although the doctor seemed disarmingly weak, with the inert look of his pale face over a plaid suit, he had moved with agility into that first open wound. Perhaps that's what he'd been waiting for.

"I'm sure Charlotte is as anxious to have this business settled as we all are. We've always wanted things together."

Else's mother looked uncomfortable, as though an old pain were beginning to spread across some inside surface. She said nothing, however.

"What do you think, Mrs. Rainer? Have you always been a team, do you think?"

She hesitated only a moment, took a long shaky breath and then said in a hushed voice, "I guess we were once that way. But —" She was careful not to look at Else's father then. The cloth of her worn winter coat lying folded across her lap seemed to give her some comfort, for that is where she was looking. "It's been changing over the years."

"And how's that, Mrs. Rainer?"

"Well, I don't trust him anymore and I have to think of the children and he pretends there's nothing wrong in front of others," she blurted out, looking alarmed because she'd started to cry much sooner than she'd wanted to. She was fumbling for a frayed kleenex in a pocket of the coat. The kleenex looked as though it had already been wept in that day.

Else's father was sucking in the skin of his cheeks tautly and he looked at her mother with undisguised anger. Or perhaps it was fear.

"She's always been a nervous woman, incapable of supporting me in my career, always undermining what I've achieved, pointing out our family problems to others. Instead of concentrating on the good things. Like the house I moved with my own two hands from Peterborough, piece by piece, so she would have comfort. She never thinks of the fact that she's had her own car for years, she has six fur coats, yes, six of them. We sail together with the family in a boat we built together. Nothing is ever enough. I have given her and the children so much; she bleeds me and then insults me by putting me in a loony bin and saying she can't trust me. Trust me!"

He was shouting, there was a strong tic in one of his wooden cheeks. Whitecaps of saliva had been whipped up on his lips.

"Don't get so excited, Mr. Rainer," the plaid-suited doctor said, as though speaking to a caged animal just out of reach. As though stroking her father through the bars. "I'm here to hear both sides. But I'm curious to see what your wife has to say about her lack of trust in you, and her idea of what's wrong.

"Has he worked hard to give you things?" the doctor asked her mother, who was still sniffling and looking as though she were heading into that cage with her husband. As his victim.

"Oh God, he's always been so materialistic. As though cars in the driveway give you happiness," she sobbed quietly. "But he doesn't mention how he picks at the kids constantly. They have to stand first in the class, not second. My God, I remember Else here had appendicitis and he didn't believe she was sick. He told her to stop feeling sorry for herself, and go outside and rake leaves."

Else looked down then, as though to the white scar looking like a little bit of railway track on the right-hand side of her abdomen. Twelve stitches.

"And I'll never forget when our oldest was being confirmed and she wore nail polish and he slapped her in the face and cut off her nails so short that all her fingers were bleeding."

The doctor suddenly looked startled and noted something in the file laid casually on his knee. Sat up straighter, straining the buttons on his plaid jacket.

"How old was your eldest when she was confirmed?" he asked, with a strange colour in his pale cheeks.

"Why, thirteen, of course. We're Lutheran . . . well, if we're anything any longer. Gerhard had a disagreement with the pastor so we don't go to church anymore." Else's mother looked fearfully toward her husband, who said nothing. His body was motionless but his eyes looked as though he were undergoing torture.

"The argument wasn't about religion," she added, "but about the building. You see, my husband designed the church. And the fight was about that, about the way the new addition was being put on the church."

"Yes, yes, I see. How old is she now, your eldest daughter?" the doctor asked, beginning to seem bland again. The flush gone from his face.

"Twenty, she's almost twenty. Oh, Gerhard has no understanding of their needs. She's in university now and you know what he did? He didn't let her have any male companionship without following her in his car. So she got married — secretly." Her mother's eyes, quite a lovely pale blue, were becoming red-rimmed and puffy with the difficulty of explanation. And she sounded too much as though she were complaining, and that was something she rarely did — complained.

Else knew her mother was feeling this counselling session was a big mistake. That there would be no easy way out of this position of accusing her husband. What good could possibly come of telling a wishy-washy shrink of their troubles? Still, Else could see it felt good. To have someone outside of the family know her fears. Know of her love for her children and for her husband. Perhaps something she could not yet imagine could come of this. Something.

Else's father had started an unnatural kind of smiling that looked like the animal in the cage was resisting the stroking. Was baring his teeth. His anger had retreated again behind the cold metal shine in his eyes and his fingers were tapping out urgent messages on the armrest of his chair.

"Let me tell you something about my Charlotte," he said through half-closed teeth. His taking fond possession of her name sounded menacing. "She sees what she wants to see. She makes me an ogre to the children so she can swing them closer to herself. She has always tried to cause this gap between me and my own children.

"She needs a lot of attention. Which I have tried to give her. But she is saying things that are untrue of me, even to my business colleagues. Everywhere she tries to gain this sympathy. And of course she has made me angry when she does this; it is as though my wife were betraying me. Of course I've been driven to hit her once or twice."

Else's father admitted that as though he had already revealed the justification for his actions. As though the doctor couldn't help but agree.

"You know why she's put me in here, of course. Else probably knows this anyway so I shouldn't be ashamed to say this terrible thing in front of my poor daughter. But Charlotte wants me out of the way so she can make eyes at the family doctor. They're in on this together. He's the one who took me out of my own house in my pyjamas on a Sunday morning in front of all the neighbours. And he's an old friend of the family's, too. An old friend," her father repeated, and his eyes looked as dangerous as light glancing on steel and his voice was stretching tight as wire.

"Oh, Gerhard, how can you say that?" Else's mother was looking with disbelief at her husband and the idea seemed to cross her mind that this man long married to her could in fact not be held responsible for what he said. That was why he was here, wasn't it? She took a much gentler tone, she even reached nervously for his hand. "Oh, Gerhard, we are all trying to help you. We don't want to lose you. We love you."

"You can see how she changes when the tables are turned, doctor. You can see how she becomes the perfect wife when she's caught with her roving eyes flirting with everyone."

"Do you think your wife is really having an affair, right now, with you in the hospital?" the doctor interrupted brusquely, catching her father off guard.

"Well . . . not really . . . no," he said slowly, as if savouring the realization. "No," and his voice had cracked suddenly.

He was close to tears and it had a terrible strangling effect on his throat and he looked so helpless. Fidelity had been cracked like a whip.

Else's mother leaned forward on her chair and looked hopeful that he might break down. In front of the doctor. So someone would believe her. So her husband would loosen some of the burden held tight as a fist close to him.

But as soon as she glanced quickly over to the doctor, whose placid eyes had not registered yes or no, belief or disbelief, her husband's story or hers, Else's father once again caught his balance on the steel wire inside his head and said, "No, but she is breaking apart our family. And my family is first, doctor. When I feel this way about my family, when I feel them going their different ways, it affects my work. And she knows this."

That's the kind of thing that happened when Else's mother went to the hospital. Else only went with her that once but she heard about all the other times. How her father would twist everything around and make it look as though he'd been hard done by. As though he'd had about as much as he could take. And her mother would always come home with puffy eyes and Else worried about her driving like that, maybe driving off the road or something when she was crying and thinking about everything. Thinking about infidelity.

How did it ever start between them? Somehow she can never even imagine her parents in the act of loving. Had she ever surprised them in that kind of passion, she would have certainly thought it to be another form of their violence together; the ragged breathing, the eyes closed or turned inward, her father pressed hard into her mother's soft body, her mother making those sounds. She would have believed it to be only another kind of suffering between them.

But she can't think when she might have come across their lovemaking, unless it might have been in those quiet afternoons, when they were asked as children to go to their rooms and take a "rest" after lunch. They were really far too old to nap by that time, but the house was always so quiet. Could they have made love that quietly?

And yet she could not imagine either of them ever having strayed from their own sorry marriage bed, looking for a different love. Yes, that was the problem, Else thinks. That the house was so quiet and that they were faithful to each other. Face to face, day to day, passing in the kitchen, in the bathroom, with only the children to keep them separate. Her father could probably sense that there were others who saw her mother differently, could have given her other things than that terrible quiet of the afternoon rests, those silent truces in their war. Yes, that made people lonely, that way of always being together. Even crazy.

Else thinks of her father constantly imagining her mother lost to another's arms; she thinks of his placing her on that terrible pedestal of infidelity and then bringing her down. Infidelity, once imagined, is like a snowfall. It starts with the tiniest snowflakes that melt if you hold them in your hand, but soon the air is thick with it, and the whiteness covers everything. Changes the way everything looks. You have to imagine what was once there. The butterfly chairs, the flowers, the picnics when you lay with your lover on the bare ground. By then it is too late. Everything or anything fits the crime. The way she looks at the mailman, the way she wears her hair parted just so, the way her skirts fall just a little longer at the back than at the front.

And no love is finally great enough to take that wayward lover back. You try and you try, like her father did, to make the lover fit the crazy love you have for her. By then no punishment is too great for the imagined infidelity.

An anxious feeling passes through Else; lights glimmer briefly before they are caught up, like distant Christmas baubles, in the snow swirling against the body of the house. Then suddenly the snow seems to be suspended, still, and the house moving faster and faster; she is fighting a feeling of inertia, of sleep pressing her against the frayed seat of the butterfly chair. She thinks, this is the way it feels when things happen. This is the way it feels when it snows, when lovers are covered with snow . . . and she falls unsteadily asleep.

Else is standing on a wide, flat stretch, which she assumes must be the place called December, and there is only the faint light of a farmhouse here and there in the distance to mark anything alive in the scene. And suddenly from nowhere the whistle and clamour of a train, approaching fast and seemingly straight for her — and passing before Else has a chance to cry out. In fact she finds herself pressing close to the cold metal body of the train rushing past, but an old man with a lantern holds her arms tightly and draws her back. By then it is too late, she can feel it; her father has gone.

Else walks slowly through the deep snow blown in drifts onto the tracks until the dead white feeling is inside her legs, her lungs, until she is part of it. She realizes she has been crying, and that she is tired, even from the walking, wanting to be absorbed into the cold white space left after the train's stormy passage. Her hair seems frozen on top; she wants to sit waist-deep in the opaqueness and lose her hard outline, dull the feeling of her burning fingers and feet in a colourless sleep.

Then suddenly she finds the stairs, climbs them wearily, one, two, three, and walks along the platform of the deserted train station. The schedule looks more like a memorial than an outline of trains running; Amelius Dakon, 1903–1979; Holden H. Adelhelm, 1896–1956; Ray Parker, who went to her school and then to Nam, 1943–1972; Lilian Prayer, may her soul with the black taffeta skirt rest gracefully on a straight-backed chair, 1912–1971. Else's hands wipe off the snow, her fingers tracing the names carved into the metal plate, which stretches like a plaque on a war memorial the length of the old station, until she finds Rainer, Charlotte and Gerhard, Still Together, 1922-1967, 1926–1967.

The old man with the lantern walks by and seems not to hear when she asks about the next train. But as he passes, the dim light from the lantern falls on the tall letters that rise above her along the roof of the station — so that is the name of this desolate place — December.

It is only then she sees three thin windows in a row, a warm light shining from them out onto the snow, and the name above the door seeming somehow familiar, The New Germany Kitchen. As she scrapes stiffly through the door with the red Coca-Cola sign, she enters a room smelling of coffee and frying; the small tables are covered with fingerprinted oilcloth, also red. The door slams behind her, drawn shut with a squeaky spring; the place is empty but for a man eating alone.

It's a dreary place, she thinks, it has the feel of leaving behind any expectations at the door. The service is bound to be slow, the food adequate — a little too heavy perhaps, but big helpings — the lampshades are greasy and a little the worse for wear, and yet all that doesn't seem to matter. The place will never change — she can feel that — and yet it draws her in like a mother's dirty apronfront to its comfort.

She finds a table in the corner; it is then she sees the snow melting in dark circles from her feet, which are bare, and she notices she is wearing only a night dress, flannel the ribbons on the shoulders drooping down with tiny strands of ice. Else can see the small eyes of the older man across the room watching her, and thinks his face, like the room itself, somehow familiar.

It seems to take forever before a waitress comes. A woman finally passes through the ragged curtain hanging behind the counter, and presses her hands flat on the table, as though resting for a moment, her red knuckles and her hairline reminding Else somehow of her mother. The woman bends to her and asks whether she'd like the special; roast pork with dumplings and sauerkraut, coffee included. Else nods, and a man with a limp and a thin, hunched back goes to a dark corner of the room and settles himself behind a very old upright piano. The notes that come out are somehow comforting, and his lips sing "Wie grün sind deine Blätter" dryly, in a kind of whisper. He pauses every now and then to sniffle and blow his nose on a forlorn cotton handkerchief, the kind her father used to pull like a sorry trick from his pants pockets.

Else smiles a thin line of recognition — of course, the song is "Oh Tannenbaum" — her father had played it at Christmas, five uncertain voices falling in with the jovial sound of the accordian on his lap. Too late she realizes her smile has seemed an invitation — one eyebrow above the old man's deep-set eyes rises and falls like the curtain before and after a very short performance. He brings his coffee cup over then and introduces himself as Carl Jung. There seems to be no point in arguing with him; she will soon know whether that's the truth.

"Just waiting for the train," she says. "Else Rainer," she adds, as though the name might ring a bell of tragedy for him. She has always assumed that Jung would require so little explanation.

But he looks puzzled and asks, "What are you doing here, Else? I haven't seen you before and I often sit here alone and read."

"I think I've had what you used to call 'forbidden thoughts,' " Else says teasingly, brushing her hand across her forehead in the way she often does when uncomfortable.

"You mustn't think those forbidden thoughts, as they seemed to me then because of the strict taboos that hung over my childhood, were anything but a source of anguish for me. I never spoke of many dreams I had in childhood until I was already an old man. The one I had of the cave —" Else blushes, remembering "— I only confided to my wife when I was sixty-five. Not before."

Else feels a little ashamed of having baited him like that.

She can feel by the small measure of loneliness he's just described in himself that this is indeed the man Jung. Although his physical appearance has shrunk somewhat, the thing that seemed so much a centre of that large man is now even more visible, is less protected by body.

Else thinks of the dreams Jung had at a very early age, of a man in black coming down a roadway, his feeling that the man in black was coming to take someone, something away. To change things forever. She wonders how long it will be before the next train arrives. It's such a quiet night she's almost sure she'll hear the whistle long before the train reaches the run-down station.

"The train might not come," he says, almost inaudibly. "Sometimes the train doesn't come. I find I read a lot of my own works over and over again," he adds.

Else is fingering the dead flowers in the vase on the table, the buds of the cornflowers break off in her hands, the dry bits of stem litter the table. "I used to play a little game with myself that I would meet you someday, in a garden. My mother was an avid gardener, you see. But she always left it looking partly overgrown, partly wild. Whether that was because she ran out of time to tend it, I don't know — I like to think the wild look of her daisies and Black-eyed Susans and morning glories was intentional. So I imagined us meeting in my mother's garden. You and I sitting in the golden butterfly chairs, facing the house. It was a very safe game, because you were so out of reach, already in the past, and I was never ready."

"Ready?" His eyebrows start their little dance once again.

"Well, I always thought that when I met you, I would at the same time, like some great crash, run into my father. And for that I had to be ready."

"I'm not certain, but I think I've spoken with your father," Jung says carefully. "He's a very interesting man, and I would even say a charming one . . ." He pauses, considering. "He talks a great deal of all the things he's accomplished; I think he's a bit adrift here. Ambition is a little misplaced now . . . well, you'll soon see what I mean. But in general they keep to themselves a lot — I haven't said more than hello to your mother — they live on a mountainside that is quite secluded. But from time to time I run into them when I'm hiking and they are always having the kind of heated, idealistic arguments you have when you're young and in love — I don't think they have ever really gotten over what happened."

"Of course they would be together still," Else says, her voice suddenly trembling, disappointed, like a child's. Her face dark. Of course — she remembers their names on the platform of the station — Still Together. "I don't know what else I expected."

For a moment they are both silent. She is trying not to believe that she will meet them like that, together. She can feel the terror of becoming a child again, wound up in the thing they are apparently still trying to outlive.

"You know what I feel right now?" Else blurts out. "That I don't want to meet them at all. At least not together. Maybe my mother in a moment away from my father, maybe my father on his territory. But, oh God, not still together." She buries her head in her folded arms on the table top, and a low, helpless sound, like the piano notes being struck again and again by the sad pianist playing Christmas music, plays over the room.

"Let me tell you a story," Jung says calmly, never moving to touch her or console her in that way. "My father died, of course, when I was still young, and several months before my mother's death, I had a dream. I went into my library, and there stood my father, looking as though he'd returned from a long journey, and looking somehow more youthful than I remembered him, without his stern look of authority which had always hung over me. I wanted to show him my house, my family, tell him all that had happened to me, but I quickly saw that my father had his mind on some problem of his own. That he was seeking, of all things, my advice.

"He said, since I was a psychologist, he would like to know more about the state of marriage. About the things that happen between two people long married. I never understood the dream until my mother died suddenly in January of the next year.

"I laughed afterward to think that my father had wanted to know more about marriage because he was preparing to resume his duties as a husband. But what startled me about the dream was that my father had obviously not gained any insights into life from his vantage point beyond it."

Else looks across the table at Jung but she does not smile, and her hands are holding the table edge as though for balance.

"I know what you are thinking," Jung says, "that the dead are possessors of great knowledge. And here you are looking at me and I am still wearing this old melton-cloth jacket with the worn-out elbows, and —" Else looks accusingly at the jacket, as though she wants to place blame and cannot think where to place it.

"But that's the thing," Jung adds with a sly smile, "more than ever now I believe that what a man brings over at the time of his death is of vital importance. So what you have imagined, Else, does in fact carry a great deal of weight. There will perhaps never be that meeting with your imagined Jung in your mother's garden, but still —"

Else's face is a net of tight lines. She is trying to think her way out of the trap she suddenly finds herself in. "I just can't believe that my father is still bragging and browbeating my mother. Of course, he has a whole new audience, doesn't he? That's wrong, though. That's wrong. Why has nothing changed?"

Suddenly the room is vibrating, the old red and black tiled floors shaking, as the train comes into the station. Else looks about nervously; perhaps the train won't stop. Perhaps it will carry on and there will be no need for her to go out once more into the cold, in her bare feet, with only a nightgown on.

Feeling so fragile and foolish, like a child who's been tricked on the subject of death.

But the train slows with a long hiss of steam, and through the foggy windows of the cars she sees that there are more passengers than places to sit. They are standing pressed together, looking out with panic-stricken faces at the station, looking somehow desperate.

There are only four teenagers standing on the platform, a cloud of cigarette smoke hanging between their faces. They move slowly into one of the cars, and there is some commotion then, a man who wants to push past them, wants off the train. There is a terrible noise of human voices when the doors open, lost again when the doors press shut, keeping the man inside, his hands pressed against the glass. Else makes no move to stand or leave the small restaurant. In fact she scarcely seems to be breathing.

But Jung has apparently heard nothing, not the train's eerie whistle, nor the ominous chuffing of the engine, the cruel clanking of the wheels. He is watching Else intently, has moved his large head forward into the lamp's light and is puffing on his pipe, as though he were preparing himself to listen. "Has it ever occurred to you that the sting of death in your parents' story might simply disappear now? Become unimportant?"

She thinks about that for a minute. Why, of course, the idea of having lost them, of it all having ended so badly, wouldn't really matter if —

The train seems to be waiting for someone. Jung gestures toward it with a long, thin arm and a large-knuckled hand, the palm open. He seems to be inviting her to get on the train with the horror-stricken faces.

Else turns her eyes away from the tall, thin windows rimmed with condensation. She desperately wants the train to leave.

A terrible series of fears begins to rise up inside her. And the first of these is that the man who has allegedly been Carl

Jung all evening might in fact be someone else. In the shadows his large nose and faded beard jutting out into space (had Jung had a beard?) are incredibly like the caricatured turn-of-the-century shrink; trained in Zurich, having practised as a young man in large, abysmal asylums of Victorian gloom, and looking formidably committed. With his heavy wool suit and his pipe, and an accent heavy as stone, good God, he could be anyone.

The second thing that occurs to her is that without death as the invisible edge there may no longer be any point in telling the truth. Keeping your nose clean, so to speak. If this man were in fact lying and leading her on, who would care? He might never have met her parents at all; he might simply be as well-read in Jung's works as she herself is.

And the third thing that occurs to her is that he might just be trying to pick her up. Have a good time. That has always been the third thing to occur to her for so many years.

"No one really knows," Jung says slowly. "It is all rumoured, the subject of endless stories, and the cause for religion, just as it was before."

Else looks startled; had he not just been suggesting that the sting of death might finally disappear? She is certain now that his talking in riddles is suspect.

"I know you are afraid once again of being disappointed, Else. I know you have been trying to discover whether I am in fact Carl Jung."

She can barely see Jung's face any longer as he leans back in his chair just outside the circle of soft light, the smoke from his pipe seeming so inviting and safe. The candle hisses a little, smelling wonderfully sweet. She hasn't even noticed the train leaving, but the sound of its whistle is already far down the tracks.

"Tell me what you have been dreaming," Jung says gently. His voice seems far away, obscured by the sounds of a midway.

"I am riding the ferris wheel," Else begins. She feels as though she's just been awoken from a deep sleep, her voice is soft and low, the words come out slowly. "When the wheel swings down and stops beside the wooden platform where the joy riders climb in and out of the seats, my father climbs in beside me. He seems in good humour and even gives my head a light touch as though I were still a little girl. We climb up in the air together, the air sharp and cold on our faces. Just as we pass the top of the circle, just as my stomach lurches slightly and we seem to drop sharply, we catch sight of my mother. The skirt of her white dress is blowing up behind her, and in the dust rising around the people moving from booth to booth my mother seems to stand out, pure and clean.

"We go around and around on the wheel, and each time we pass the spot where the wheel drops sharply my stomach flies up against my ribs, my eyes catch sight of my mother in the white dress, and my father smiles. His eyes shine with warmth. His thinning hair is flying up from his forehead, making him look somewhat comical.

"I place my hand over his as the wheel goes down once more. I can see tears rolling down his cheeks. It may be the wind whipping his eyes, but I don't think so somehow. And suddenly he says, 'I wish I could take your mother into the Alps again on my motorcycle; she used to hold my waist so tightly as though she were afraid. But glad that I was there to hold. I had to drive very fast to make her hold me like that.'

"Suddenly I can feel the danger. I want off the ferris wheel next time around, but I know I am meant to enjoy the ride for as long as my father intends. 'Listen, I know Mutti loves you. And I don't think she's ever thought of leaving you,' I say, shocked that I can imagine my mother leaving my father.

"But my voice is lost in the air, which swooshes past us, for he doesn't even hear me. His eyes are far away, searching the fairgrounds. Suddenly he wants the wheel stopped, he stands up in his seat. I feel we may fall and I clutch frantically to his waist, to his belt, trying to bring him back down.

"Then we are falling together, my father and I. We are both falling, but suddenly I am alone. Without him.

"I am suddenly in the house of my childhood. Except it is plain that my father has been living here alone — it is a terrible mess. Yes, and I feel as though I am somehow a visitor. Even an intruder. In fact my father isn't at home. There is just an empty house that feels full of his fears and his dreams and his leftover parts of things. And I have a horrible feeling that the worst has happened.

"In what seems to be the living room — have I grown up here? — there are the ribs of a boat, curving from ceiling to floor around the furniture pushed together in the centre of the room. Where the heating vents once were there are now huge gaping holes that seem to call for parts of bodies, or at least articles of sacrifice. And sure enough, when I look down one of the openings I see that he's stuffed it full of money, and the house is filled with the slightly fleshy smell of money growing warm from the furnace heat. I go to the thermostat and turn the furnace up — the money blows gently out of the vents and into the room. A few of my father's hard-earned dollars at a time.

"There is food on the table in the next room, as though the table has been set for four, no five, many times and still no one has arrived. Or stayed long enough to eat. There are small plates and large plates, all clean, soup bowls, wine-glasses, knives and forks set in the European fashion, and all untouched. There are the decayed remains of a salad, the fruit browned and the air sweet with its rotting, and there is a loaf of dark rye as hard as a rock.

"I look for signs of my father's sleeping. That seems important to find out. Again it looks as though he has tried to sleep here and there, all without success; the floor has been tried, a pillow lying there with a small hollow where his head has been. A cushion from the sofa has been placed in the bathtub and a blanket still remains in a puddle on the floor. He's rested his head wearily against lampshades, on book cases, even on the stairs leading down to the basement. And everywhere he's placed his head, there remains an imprint.

Sometimes his profile, more often a vague shape not unlike the ultrasound pictures of unborn babies. The only place that hasn't been slept in is their old bed, my mother's and father's. The covers are pulled up tight and not a finger has rested here.

"I go to his study next, am drawn to it. And yet I'm afraid, for more than anywhere else in the house he seems to remain in this room. This is the place where he has brought everything to pass, I think.

"There are several books lying open on the drafting table. One is *The Family Altar*, a book we read together on Sundays, less and less after we stopped going to church. But there are apparently no words of advice left for my father in his hour of greatest need; the pages are blank. As though the text has been erased.

"There is also a thin red volume, leather-bound. It is a photo album I've never seen. And I don't recognize the people in the photos at first. The pictures are in the sepia tone of early photographs and the people are very posed. I suppose the soft-faced woman with the sad smile to be my father's mother. People have said that I look like her. But the boy with the patent-leather shoes, white ankle socks, short pants, frilly white shirt, and the long golden hair? Is that my father? His eyes are so soft, just like his mother's, but not so full and round. They are eyes that should be protected from seeing too much. Perhaps that's why his mother is holding him around the middle as he stands before her.

"The third book is covered in a plain brown paper jacket with no writing on it at all. As I lift the cover the paper crackles as though with electricity. I leap back, my skin is hot and stings as though it's been burned. The book — I lean over it this time without touching it — is called *Kleine Geschicte von Alchemie*, by Hans Lichtung. Alchemy? Once my father looked for water on our property by using a bent willow branch that looked like a giant wishbone from a chicken carcass. He walked, head down, over the entire uncleared plot of land, through the swamp, past the clumps of sumac bushes, over the slight rise where the dog was later buried, to the elm tree that marked the western edge of the acreage. And then back. 'The branch will quiver,' he said.

"And of course at New Year's we used to have the huge pot with boiling water, and we'd drop the lead in, the sizzling would carry on for a few minutes, and the shapes lifted out were our fortunes for the next twelve months, the shape of the year to come. Once mine looked like a rabbit and my brother's looked like an axe or a boot. My mother's always came out looking like flowers. And my father would laugh at any shape he fished out of the steaming pot and say that he'd inherited the wrong luck. Someone else's luck. He'd say that every year.

"That family tradition had seemed like magic; none of the other kids at school had ever known what I was talking about when I described it. So I imagine my father has been practising a kind of magic, turning the upside-down house with his misplaced objects into some sort of gold.

"There's an odd smell in his room; not the dust, not simply the stale darkness. The smell is vaguely like incense in a church. And then I see them — eight small blackened copper bowls filled with ashes, all in a row. The ashes are not grey but pinky brown, and they smell like blood. Smell salty sweet and seem ominous.

"I feel like screaming . . . I scream . . . I scream . . . I scream . . . I seem to be pushing through a dark curtain, which clings to my face and is smothering me. When I finally part the heavy curtain, I look back; behind me is a small secretive booth looking somewhat like a tawdry fortune teller's, with a sign propped up next to it, which says 'Dare to step inside and see what the future holds.'

"I seem to be once again back at the fairground. But it is empty and it is winter. Things have not been packed up, there are still tents flaps stirring from the people who once passed the games and the exhibits of pies and quilting. Hot dog vending machines and cotton candy booths are here and there, the animals abandoned in their prize-winning pens of slaughter look mournful and too fat. The rabbit that won first prize looks as though it may say something to me, and then turns away. There is a fine covering of snow on everything, even on the refuse; the cardboard Cracker Jack cartons and the popsicle sticks snap and squirm beneath my feet.

"My family has gone. I know that and yet I walk around the place as though it holds some special memory for me. I go to the ferris wheel because that has always been my favourite ride. And then I know why I have come.

"To someone else it might have looked like a woman making angels in the snow, her arms outstretched, her face and chest absorbed in white. The woman is wearing a white dress and I know her face. But there are small specks of red, which make her look as though someone has thrown red confetti over her in a moment of celebration.

"But no, oh no, suddenly the small specks are windmilling blood, blood flies like the veil of a bride over her face and gently over her shoulders. To me it looks like the woman in the white dress has fallen (or perhaps she's been pushed) from the ferris wheel in the dead of winter."

Else watches the man named Jung carefully. He begins to smile and his eyebrows never move at all.

"Else, I know you feel yourself to be responsible. But Else, if you are ever going to feel free enough to marry —"

"Marry?" Else thinks of the woman in the white dress, a feeling of tension in her stomach. It is almost painful, like the gentle warning months before a violent birth. "Marry?" she asks again, in a hushed voice.

And he tilts his face forward into the pale sunlight coming suddenly through the windows of the small restaurant, and for a moment she thinks the face might be Dean's. And he laughs, as true a laugh as she has ever heard.

PART IV

The Letter

She fingers the two bits of evidence — the letter and the slides of the fair-haired woman in red with the smudged black eyebrows. The woman scarcely recognizable as her mother. She throws it all into the fire.

She can scarcely bring herself to watch the slides of her mother burning there slowly, too slowly, in the fire she's built with the few sticks of kindling that remain. The celluloid of the slides seems to take forever to curl, makes the image of her mother parading like that for her father disappear as though she were still melting for him, even after all these years. This is the underside of the thing about strict families, she thinks bitterly. Where had her mother gotten that short red thing with the low neckline? Had she sewn it with the same machine she'd used to smock their dresses for school and sew their matching coats as children? Had she made that thing just to please her father?

How could she have done that, her own mother? How could she have put all that black makeup around her eyes, making herself look so tired and so indecent? That's the word that keeps occurring to her. The thought of her mother lifting her leg just so in the black net stocking to give her father a thrill makes her feel sick. She resents that this could have happened after the letter; twenty years later her father had talked her mother into the tight red dress, putting her in front of the camera in the worst possible light after all the children were asleep.

The letter is burning much more quickly than the later things, than the guilt-ridden pictures of the two once in love stooping to any prop to keep the fires burning. The letter is illustrated on the borders with the flowers and small animals her mother had drawn in a dreamy fashion on the flyleaves of all her old books as well. The letter is folded and bound with a red ribbon, which has held the message intact even after a world war and several moves across oceans and continents. The letter makes her even more ashamed for her mother than the slides. Because the letter shows that she once believed in something so strong with her husband that she chose to quote a famous German poet on the subject of loving and send it open-hearted like that, when she found she was pregnant in wartime.

A strip of the letter begins to stir and spiral up into the air, lands on the hearth, refuses to burn. She translates the German unwillingly; "Sex is difficult, yes. Men have made even eating into something else." A small breeze from the fire lifts the charred paper into the air for a moment, dropping it once more onto the coals, her mother's words almost gone. ". . . people misuse this experience . . . tired spots of their lives, as distraction . . . instead of a movement toward high moments." Else smiles a thin line of recognition. They are famous lines from a series of letters the best-loved German poet had written as a young man. Her mother had copied them in a careful hand and sent them to a man who all those years misunderstood and grew angry.

She remembers her mother reading from the Rilke book one day when she had just returned from school. Her mother was ironing, the small book with the watermarked purple cover propped open against the bread box on the table. There was the smell of freshly washed cottons, her mother's cheeks were flushed from the heat, a fringe of fair hair falling over her brow as her arm swooped down the ironing board and back. Every now and then she turned a page, slamming the iron down hard on a shirt-sleeve, the steam rising while she murmured a line or two from that small book. Else had asked her mother questions about love then; it became an afternoon of quiet advice. Her mother always gave quiet advice, as though she were half afraid her good intentions would turn out wrong.

Strange that she should be destroying the few things that remain, performing a kind of alchemical ritual, leaving only ashes. Of course it was never the colour of gold that mattered in alchemy (although many alchemists were martyred by that misunderstanding, being imprisoned or beheaded by kings and worldly patrons), but the process of imagination. A hot light from the fire plays over the mothball-smelling shawls and scarves, the clumsy costume necklaces, the hole punch from her father's study, one of his slide rules, and two photographs, all seemingly carefully arranged on the hearth before her. She sits naked, cross-legged, in the butterfly chair.

In one of the photographs she is perhaps five, crouched forward in the protective deep lap of the same butterfly chair she has carried with her all these years, the canvas brilliant yellow then. She is playing dominoes with a young woman in a stylish fifties' ponytail — her mother. It is doubtless an event staged for her father's countless photos of family life, her mother once again supplying him with the images he needed. Else peers at the other photo, somewhat crinkled; she is even smaller in this picture. She supposes her father has posed her with the new puppy, and she is leaning away from the eager black face, his pink tongue flying like a flag, her own face screwed up with distaste. Else can sense that the photo is intended to be a record of the gift she was given by her father.

To Else the pictures are evidence of the feeling she'd always had of being peripheral in the family, at the edge, as though her father were the central image. Even though her father was the one taking the shots, he was always very much the subject of the scenes. He was what it was all about.

There are many times she has longed for photos of her father. Other than the ones in his boyhood, with the silly blond curls and the short pants, black patent-leather shoes. Or the few that once remained of his time in the army, looking long and thin in his uniform, aping manhood and smiling sheepishly, all lost now. She has often wanted one way to remember him that is not defined by a feeling of having lost him. Yes, that has always been the secret; the fact that she could never really reach him. Just as she was about to inherit her own separate sense of him, he disappeared, leaving an empty space so pervasive she has never been able to imagine life without him.

Else tries to remember the letters she wrote to him, what she would have tried to say to her father while he was in hospital. For even that time is marked and vivid because of his absence.

Dear Father:

(it must have been "father"; she had never been as familiar with him as the kids who simply called out, "Hi, Dad!" when their fathers rolled up in their cars)

I have been using the old Kodak you gave me and had my first thirty-six pictures developed yesterday. I have mounted all the better ones in a book so you can see what happened while you were away. So that maybe it will be as though you weren't away from home at all.

(then something of Martin's birthday, which had been a sad day because she had been thinking only of her father, stuck in that grim hospital, behind bars)

Things sure do look different in black and white. Even

Martin seems less my brother and more a character in some story. He's always throwing something or falling or looking surprised — remember how he got that fishhook caught in the back of his head last summer when he was just learning to cast? And you had to bandage his head with that ripped-up bed sheet, making him look so sick and wounded, so that some car on the highway near our anchored boat would pick you both up and take you to the hospital? And Thor looks younger somehow, as though he were still a pup. I guess it sort of exaggerates everything. You'll have to explain why that happens when we have some time together again in the darkroom.

She can't remember at all how she must have finished the letter. There is something out of place; Else can sense it. The memory of the dog is somehow suspect.

And suddenly Else knows. She knows the dog had died long before her father was in hospital. He was no longer there, for example, walking alongside her like a shadow on the passage to and from school the winter she was eight. The winter that might have been any other winter in Canada in the late fifties. The winter that fell on a small, six-room school just north of Toronto looking like so many other schools then just outside of Perth, Hamilton, or Peterborough. But there is one day in that winter that rises up so suddenly inside her, that is so distinct and so fixed in her memory, that it will probably be discovered in her after her death as actual and apparent as a thin white scar shielding a chipped bone in her knee.

It was the lunch hour and mist was rising from the cold landscape where the sun had warmed things a little. Here and there circles of exposed earth looked like dark wounds in the covering of snow. Five or six overgrown lugs of boys still in grade eight stood midway between their homes and the school, hunching their shoulders angrily against both the cold and the grim prospects of their lives. Some of them had forgotten which grade they were in, for they rarely entered the school. Once, when Les Arnold had been asked by the short, very bald principal to attend school more frequently and promptly, Les had grabbed the small man by the collar of his shirt, shaking him like a terrier worrying a rat.

An eight-year-old girl walked across the winter's scene and was passing the boys now, her thin legs like sticks against the banks of snow beside the ditches. These were the boys who stood in a huddle beside the skating rink Saturdays, eyeing the girls who were older than she was. And these were the boys her mother had told her stole cars and started grass fires in the summer. She recognized John Large, who sometimes smiled at her and wore a lumberjack shirt, and Peter Topper, who never smiled at anyone and wore a black leather jacket. Once her mother had met one of the boys coming down the path in the heavy bush behind the house. It was after dusk. Her mother had come into the house laughing at how he was whistling and talking to himself as he passed her on the path. "He was probably as afraid of the dark as I was," she'd said.

Still, the girl was careful not to look at the boys directly or walk too near them.

One spat into the white snow as she drew near, another reached an arm out and grabbed the girl roughly by the hood of her coat. In an instant she was lying on the ground, those great hulking boys looking down and laughing.

"Do you know that you're a Nazi's daughter?"

"Do you like your father?"

"I'll bet you'll wear black boots in a few years and torture guys — take their balls off."

"Yeah, she'll press them slowly in a vice," said John Large, holding himself in the crotch in mock pain. Then he hitched up his pants sharply and leaned forward over the girl — "Or maybe she'll just teach school."

Great puffs of warm air rose as the boys laughed about that.

"Spread her legs, Johnnie. I'll bet German girls are nice and tight to fuck."

"For Christ's sake, Clifford. She's just a kid. She doesn't even have tits yet."

"Yeah, but she's the German's kid."

They spat on her then, in turns, rubbing snow down her back as she squirmed soundlessly. They lifted huge slabs of ice, marbled with mud from the roadside, and dropped them on her. She merely grunted, her eyes closed, breathing loudly. When they kicked her she could hear their heavy winter boots thudding into her thin shoulder blades and down her back. They squealed with excitement when she finally screamed. She curled up in the snowbank, her mittened hands covering the back of her head.

She was late that day for lunch. As she came in the door, scraping her boots on the sill, dragging one leg awkwardly, her mother and father turned around to reproach her for dawdling on the way home from school. "When you only have an hour for lunch, Else," her mother started gently, and then stopped. Her father's typically grim face grew yet more intense and haggard as he took in her torn woolen stockings, her scratched face puffy with cold and crying, the anger beginning in his daughter's eyes. An accusation in his daughter's eyes. She asked her father then what a Nazi was.

His eyes narrowed. Her mother held the plate of dumplings and sauerkraut close to her body for comfort. Suddenly he reared up from the table, his thighs hitting the table edge, the dishes all chattering furiously. Mother and daughter moved closer together, watching the pulse in his neck as he shouted in German about the hoodlums who had done this to his daughter, and cursed the country he lived in. Cursed Canada.

"So this is a free country," he said in a whisper, one wave

of his anger subsiding. Turning and saying he didn't want lunch. Retreating with a grey face into his study.

"How can I eat," he screamed some minutes later beyond his closed door, "when my children . . . I've worked my fingers to the bone to put food on the table, to put clothes on their backs, and now, now my children are no longer safe on the street!"

Her mother took her to the bathroom then and gently removed her clothes, washing her scrapes with the iodine soap and shaking her head, her eyes brimming with tears. The girl's left knee was badly swollen. She would have to call the doctor. The school.

"Come and eat," she said finally, wearily. Believing in the ritual of restoring normal gestures to a terrible day.

When the girl shook her head and started to wail, making the low, horrible sound an animal trapped in some small dark space might make, her mother held her close and looked over the sobbing child to her kitchen table with the untouched food and the chairs pushed back.

She carried the girl to her room then and told her to sleep. "Sleep is what you need," she said.

The girl didn't return to school that afternoon and instead of sleeping she listened to her father's anger as he slammed drawers and heaved books in the room directly below her. Finally there was silence in the house of the German, an unnatural silence.

Several times that day the small girl was heard sobbing in her room and her mother rushed to her then to hold her close and tell her how things would change. How it would all seem better the next day. "Why is he so angry?" she whispered to her mother, half afraid her father would hear their voices through the old wooden floors. First those boys out of nowhere, even smiling John Large, and then her father. In spite of her mother's love, the next days and weeks and years seemed full of anger and betrayal.

"Hush now, Else. I think your father's sleeping."

Some years later, her father took her aside and set her on his knee, and said, as though referring directly to that unforgotten day of winter: "My father was a schoolteacher. As students we were asked, we were expected, to report on his remarks. Even his own children were asked to inform on their father, should he say anything critical of Hitler, or the country. Of course we were never told that we wouldn't have seen our parents again, had we said anything to the authorities. Had we not loved our parents enough in the moment. Had we doubted them. Never doubt your parents, Else. Your country may let you down. But never doubt your parents."

If she stands back from the memory, she becomes simply an eight-year-old girl in a filmstrip of the realities that remain after war. She is merely a victim, her family a small group of people irrevocably bound to a man forever out of step, a man who seemed a caricature of an entire people, angry, distrustful, and most of all, guilty. Then sometimes she can see what they saw, those hoods on a winter road who first called her father "the German."

She knows she intended to write to him while he was in hospital, but the careful weighing of the words, that must have made her hold back. She could neither have admitted to missing him nor have failed to refer to his suffering there. It would have been a trap to write to him — she sees that clearly now. Yes, writing to her father would have been an admission of her guilt. And a betrayal of her mother.

So it seems she never wrote those letters to her father at all. The truth is harder to reach, or even avoid, than she has ever imagined, Else thinks.

She will write to him now. Now when she can finally feel his pain and how it was never right. How nothing fit. How even a child sitting on his lap might have been a burden or a warning. She will write the explanation she has intended for so many years. She will admit now, finally, that it was she who called the police that morning in November when she was thirteen. That it was his daughter, Else, who turned him in.

It would be silly of me to say that I feel left behind. That after all the days I looked up to you, tried to please you, that you suddenly moved ahead of me to a dark place where no daughter can follow. Usually children are left behind to inherit the things of their parents, so they may in turn pass them on, but these deaths you left me, now what am I supposed to do with them, I have asked myself so many times.

That's just the kind of thing that would make you angry, isn't it? That you are still misunderstood. You would say that you left me so much. And yet I cannot once again reassure you that you are right; it seems much too late for that. Then what am I to write of? And how shall I speak to you? As "Vati?" A man always so fierce, so forbidding, a man I feared as a child; now, finally, shall I call you Vati? Shall I admit such profound love? The kind of love a daughter might have had before she had learned to be so careful, so wary? Shall I grant you as great a love as I give to the woman I called "Mutti"?

It's true, the good memories belong to her. Although she claimed less of our devotion, I don't feel cheated now by her illusion. Whenever I still indulge some early memory of Mutti bending to us as children (a memory sharp as broken glass), laughing with us, showing us something young and willing in herself, I do not draw back sharply, as with you. There is only the pain of having lost her before she was real, and perhaps a nagging doubt that we did not love her enough at the time.

Days we found her stooping over her gardens, with that straw hat, her hair falling over her face, she looked somehow as though she belonged with us, just because she seemed misplaced. The woman off balance when she was among us, laughing too much, too eager to please, seemed somehow more complete when viewed like that from a distance. In fact, when she straightened up from her flower beds, and the light glanced across her shoulders and her long hair, she seemed to belong to a place far removed from the hardships of her family . . . she seemed suddenly a tall woman. Then we would see a tall woman dreaming on those garden paths. Alone.

Sundays, when the bold yellow butterfly chairs framed that same woman in the old-fashioned girlish dresses you insisted on her wearing, when her three children surrounded her in whispers, leaning awkwardly into the eye of the camera, when you ran from your tripod to come into focus with us, hissing as you ran, "Smile! Look happy!" she did look happy. Tragically happy. Like a woman on an illusive holiday that's gone on far too long, being photographed with an adventurer and their three accidental children. That's what I thought.

And when she moved out of those golden chairs, never once using the power of that image, when she moved out of those chairs, always looking back over her shoulder to care for us, to clothe us, to feed us, to keep things in their proper places, she was always drawn back to the centre of that thing our family became. She was never able to walk farther away from it all than her gardens. Her gardens formed the boundaries.

Mutti in the garden; there she was never considered stupid and there her ability to adapt to the conditions you set out for her, season to season, was simply the ability to grow. To stay alive. Look beautiful and smell good while she was at it, like the flowers. There, in the garden, she learned her art.

So early evenings were the happiest time of day for her — did you know that? — because she could work with her flowers. In spite of the humid summers Toronto dished out, the mosquitoes snatching at her with open mouths, she looked happy. Then she did not seem connected to the butterless, soapless, dreamless, potato-skin years of the war, or to the later reality of raising children with a raging man in a foreign country. There, with her fingers in the black soil, all her troubles came to rest in the soft patting of the dirt around the bulbs, in the slender hope that the morning glories would climb the trellis with the blue bells facing east, that the rain wouldn't smash the raucous sunflower heads bobbing like idiots, that all would presumably grow and blossom and fall in autumn with a gentle curving of water and light like a rainbow she created.

There, in the garden, the work was gentle work, the weeds resisted only a little to their quick deaths, the flowers nestled or leaned away from her with reasons that were understandable. Their mutations and surprises were never as chilling as the changes that made her house seem bare, her children whining and restless, her vows of marriage dangerous. There the plants paid close attention to her steady hands, quiet and patient in their touch, they breathed in what she breathed out. There she held sway and had the beautiful illusion of control; whatever she planted would take its eventual shape except for summer hailstorms, or feet cutting corners on the garden paths. In the garden there was reward for time taken, care given, even if the variables of nature could take a blossom or a bed of marigolds slightly outside her reach. In the garden she had a home for her thoughts of the three children, the poems of Rilke she still read like a schoolgirl, the letters she would write to the few family members remaining in Germany. There she would often squat in her bleached-out shorts until long after dark had taken away the scene of garage, weeping willow, the cruel lights going on in the rooms of her children. With a shudder she would finally come to the house, leaving her small love of self out there in the garden.

Sure, Mutti had her flaws, but nothing too serious, even in the miserly rememberings of a child. She did herself more harm than anything I can think to blame her for. Of course I was jealous sometimes of her goodness, and still am. My school friends would sometimes confess their secrets to her, things they hadn't even told me. Then she would admit shyly to the slim sheets of poetry and painting she kept behind the iron and the sleeve board in those battered kitchen cupboards. Those things she kept as companions more delicate and loyal and hopeful than her own family. I would be surprised each time to find that of course my mother possessed like talents to the ones we were constantly applauding in you. Of course.

I know why you loved her. Every man wanted her for his own. In fact she was the kind of woman no one could leave. Your friends, even the bread man, the few classmates we were allowed to bring home, everyone wanted to stay and talk with Mutti. She gave them some sense of self-possession they otherwise lacked; the bread man became less of a loud-mouth in a Weston Breads uniform, and more contemplative, changed in her presence — "That's just fine," he would say, if she was a few cents short on her bill. He looked like a boy again, like the son every man dreamed of having, not like the bread man. That's why you had to do what you did, I guess.

Yes, it was easy to love my mother. The more surprising thing is that she loved you. And that is one of the good things I know about you. That my mother loved you. For I believe that she only cared about people who were capable of coming clean. I used to think that was just about everybody. I don't think so, not anymore.

Yes, she floats perfectly on the surface of memory now, a woman with eyes like bright blue water. Eyes that lapped at the small, dark stones of our bad deeds as children, smoothing them with her love, her love especially strong when we were wrong.

I remember Martin, pale as a boy about to lose his father, insisting that it wasn't him that broke into the neighbour's house, leaving a trail of cookie crumbs and smoked cigarettes. Probably looking into the bathroom cupboards and around the beds for signs of awkward adult life, for evidence of sex or loneliness. He insisted on his innocence for days, poor kid, and ate very little, Mutti actually believing him.

Even though there'd been no real harm done — a small

latch on the basement window had been broken — the nervous woman next door wanted an investigation. She would hold the packets of matches in her hands and complain to my mother, "The kids could have burned the house down, you know. And how do I know it was just kids?" she'd say, wide-eyed at the possibility of something worse. I think she may have simply been avenging the loneliness her fat and friendless son had to endure, and was asking some other kid to pay.

When you came home Martin ran and hid behind the red mailbox on the street corner, his lanky legs sticking out in the small space beneath if you looked hard for him. You said how it was all Mutti's fault in being so kind and so generous in her raising of the children, although you did not use those words exactly. And then you chased her around the house, hitting her again and again just after the police had made their report and gone away.

In retrospect I'd say my mother's biggest flaw had been in her love for you when you no longer deserved it.

And yet this is where the psychiatrists would all point out that it was not a question of my mother cutting her losses, or you deserving love. They were always muttering something about mental illness. You had been anxious, disturbed, although they could never agree on the precise name of your disorder. In their pale voices you had been classified as many men — a classic manic depressive, a probable paranoid schizophrenic, an interesting character disorder, as a mere workaholic, as a brittle personality with bouts of psychosis. You had struggled with a question of values common among immigrants of that generation. And European men were harder on their wives as a rule. Your wartime experiences had remained with you in a grim fashion. You had an authoritative personality. Men of genius often walked a tightrope between reality and insanity. And on and on . . . .

I had believed it too. At one time I told my friends you had been sick. Sick, I used to say, making the low and helpless sound of sympathy that admitted how close we all were to the condition of acting out our revenge on the world. We should empathize, I would add. Knowing that empathy was impossible. My friends had all had the kind of parents that stood somewhere off in the background and could be seen as small figures mowing the lawn or calling listlessly to their children. So I always reminded my friends that you had been a hero.

Remember the puppet theatre he built? I would say to those who might have sat cross-legged before the performances of "White Dog Meets the Witch" or "Hocus Pocus." Those had been among our two most shining moments in theatre. Sometimes our plays would have the backdrop of a faint green hillside leading up to a castle in the distance, sometimes we used the background of a window with curtains blowing in and a faint hint of sunshine beyond. There were gnarled trees that formed the wings on the stage for any Gothic scenes of mystery or magic forests, there were carpets that rolled back, and trap doors, and small chandeliers that twinkled mischievously with real light in them. My father had thought of everything, I used to say.

Mutti would serve lemonade to the audiences and we used to charge a quarter admission for the shows. That had also been your idea.

But still I could see it was hard for my friends to show sympathy for you, a man who had watched our earliest stories of good and evil played with the same four marionettes — the crow-faced witch with the crisp black skirt, the small white dog made of rabbit fur, a naïve-looking Rapunzel, and a needle-nosed, cherry-cheeked Pinocchio — and who had later taken the cruel moral of the stories into his own hands.

There are different rules for heroes, I insisted so many times. Explaining to the other kids, with a certain aloofness, that one pays a price for living too close to a man who can imagine almost anything and has his whole family living in that wide country. Imagine, I would say to my friends, their foreheads furrowed, their eyes retreating to their own safer childhoods, imagine the kind of afternoon when it's raining too hard to go outside, or you're stuck inside for days with a cold. My father didn't believe in television or coddling yourself, I would say — so imagine that here he stepped in with one of his ideas. One of his ideas to make you survive.

I forget how old I was or how bedridden or bored when you rigged up the telegraph throughout the house and had us talk to you only in Morse code. Had your children tapping out messages to you on the small black keys. Telegraph? my friends all asked at once, incredulous. A little afraid. Not understanding. Had he ever heard of intercom? Not the same thing for my father, I answered back. Defending you. Defending my father for his ideas.

It is difficult, I have finally realized, years later, to sympathize with the sickness of heroes.

Of course there were things I never told my friends about those afternoons of rain or sickness when we talked to you in code, as though you were miles away behind enemy lines. Positioned as we were throughout the house, on the fronts of your war. How we dreaded the things you would ask us, the impossible things, while your fingers rang staccato through the wires. Partly it was the fear of never knowing what would happen next and partly it was the fear that the idea would take over and we would be subject to playing the proper part in the drama and playing it well. Until God knows when. Our signals were slow and unsure; we longed for the end of the messages. For a power failure. For a neighbour to come calling unannounced. But none of those things ever happened. There were always more dots, dashes, pauses. We would imagine your face somewhere above or below us in the rambling old house and answer shyly, only to realize we had said the wrong things.

One day in particular stands out. It must have been the last day of the Morse-code phase; after this I remember only that you packed up the transmitters, tore the wires angrily away from the baseboards, and that was the end of it. These things usually ended bitterly. We called it the last day of the war.

It was one of those days we'd been at it for hours, not even stopping for lunch. We were tired and we were desperate; your energy seemed to be propelling us beyond the limits of endurance. You would teach us everything there was to know about communication by suppertime, you insisted. The best way was simply talking back and forth, as though it mattered, you said. Losing patience with us finally because we'd had to quit our posts for bathroom visits, because we were thirsty, hungry. Getting dizzy with concentration. "Pretend that it's a life-and-death situation," you said. "You'll get a second wind then. Then you'll start to use your brains." Dot dot dot dot pause dot dash dot dot pause dot dash dash dot rang the current in waves through the rooms. "Help," you had asked us that day, just as it was growing dark outside the windows.

Martin and I laughed nervously, whispering back and forth, "No, we can't say that. He'd get mad." There was no answer. Only silence. We hadn't been old enough to have the sympathy you required then. For you it had been a matter of survival to play the game well and our slight errors (for this is what you imagined them to be) had been a disappointment. You could feel the answers flowing through the fingers of your children and vanishing into thin air.

It was for your children, you said, that you built a race-car track running through the entire basement from the laundry room to the darkroom where a red light posed a hellish warning over the door and we heard the ominous sloshing of poisonous liquids in flasks and stained rubber pans. There you developed the scenes from life that you had created with so much abandon. There is an old home movie of me pouring water from a Coke bottle over Martin's blond head and Martin getting incredibly angry, chasing me up the beach on the Bay of Quinte and throwing shells at my thin, retreating backside. You had set up the whole thing to happen that way, and Martin was embarrassed later. And I'd cut my feet on the rocks while running away.

So when you weren't driving the droning plastic cars

around the track — and you liked to win, even when there was more at stake for the pale faces of your children who had yet to inherit your skills — then you would play virtuoso piano or old accordion tunes meant to draw your family in an ancient circle of music around you. You told folk tales in many languages, laughing at the sad quality of truth in their endings of death and misfortune, and you knew the long and difficult answers to any enquiry about the bodies of water or the relative places of art, philosophy, or the stars. To question you the night before a school project was due was like taking a trip I couldn't afford; I got the information, but I felt tired the next day, and changed by the experience. And then when the marks were due, you wanted to know how you had done. Or that is almost how it seemed. You were disappointed and clearly threatened by any mark less than A-plus. Yes, you knew, as if by heart, the histories of the words bloodshed, banking, or biopsy. One year you mastered the clarinet and auto mechanics, the next it was figure skating and the Hindi languages. Watching you had been an education in itself. A marvel. An intimidation, unless I was bound and determined to keep up.

And yet the doctors all say that it is something they have yet to discover in the sweat of schizophrenics, in the urine of the depressed, that will give us the empathy we need for such a man. So we will no longer pity you, discard you, cease to love you as we love ourselves. Only then will we finally stay in touch with a man who made his own life and those surrounding him unpeopled and unrelenting. Hooray — then the daughters of such a man will rightfully inherit not only the width of his cheekbones, the size of his nose, the shape of his hand, his health and longevity, but will also be able to follow closely in the heroic footsteps of deception, of dangerousness, of despair.

Perhaps I have tried too strenuously to keep up. In any case, your sickness has a different meaning for me now. It is no longer the memory of a man who could not succeed as plainly as he wanted and who could have been different. Who could have stopped rebelling against the small failures we others live dumbly with, year in and year out. Let him remain as he was, I say now, a genius in kid's clothing. A man who felt more pain and anguish in a day than we of good mental health feel in a lifetime. A man who invariably threw temper tantrums around his latest invention. Let him go down in our family's history with his moods intact, those dark changes in himself that only he could transform, and release like pale white doves for our forgiveness and applause. For we did applaud. We were continually won over by your strong belief that the world revolved around you. Let the doctors not take that away from us now. After all we suffered.

Oh, I do feel sympathy with you, but not in the way they intend it. The doctors want a cold, clean and, let's face it, self-saving look at bad husbands and fathers. But the kind of sympathy I feel is different. I feel it when I look in the mirror and I seem to be always a little too thin, a little gaunt in the cheeks; that kind of thinness makes people uneasy. And I live with this kind of hunger, and I eat a great deal, it's true, but the hunger remains and I see in others' eyes that I play with my hair endlessly and that it's bothering them. The way I'm twirling strands around sweaty fingers. And I realize it is summer and I hate the easiness of summers. When I should feel full and sun-warmed, content, like an animal, or like the ads of people laughing too much on picnic blankets, their faces shining as though filled with gold. Those long evenings of light are not freedom, but a burden. Like the feeling I had as a child, leaning on my handlebars in those endless summer nights when I didn't want to go home. Surely that is how you felt during the summer. I think you chose sailing as a way to make summers more difficult, cramped, tipping crazily to one side, tiring, fingers chafed and faces windburned. I think you had to invent a way to get through summers, and your dreams of going around the world were a way to leave summers behind. Find ice floes, dangerous Atlantic storms.

But it grows worse. The sympathy grows stronger in the autumn. When I look out and see my neighbours raking leaves, it hits me like a numbing pain behind the eyes. That is something I don't want to see, that hopeless gesture of persons bending and placing leaves from that whole long year into green plastic bags, suffocating parts of trees like that and then paying people to cart them away. As children we waited until winter, pretending the dead leaves were landed fish from some receding ocean, and we speared them cheerfully with pointed sticks, piling them onto our toboggan. Taking them away to the small ponds and streams of melting snow, and setting them free. I want to scream when people rake leaves, and that's when I think of your anger. Your anger about little things, as the doctors would say.

But the way I feel about winter, that must be the greatest form of sympathy for you, for the thing they name your sickness. I even think snow is beautiful and clean-looking and quiet, as opposed to the people who complainingly shovel the stuff and press it into shapes around their driveways. Shapes that will only melt in the end and lead to inquests in the spring. And I never (or almost never) hear screams when flakes fall in those country Christmas-card scenes, and I pass by the children I see here and there making the shapes of angels in the formal white covering, looking for all the world like happy carcasses, frozen in their youth, still fluttering in their hope. And I smile at them. I seem content to know that things finally end. That people lie down (or are pushed) and play at becoming angels. That is the sympathy I share with you. And that is the very thing I fear.

When I look back it seems there had always been seasons to your anger, as though the years's end was the time you had chosen for things to come right for you. It seems I can only recall sporadic incidents of rage in spring and summer, then a menacing and steady feeling of the ending like the sound of the leaves dropping from the trees in fall, building to an unbearable frenzy of something yet unfinished in your life, something requiring explanation, requiring blame, by Christmas. And that last Christmas, perhaps you too had played the gambling game, making a promise to yourself that your family would appear, as though willed by yourself, on that horizon. Giving yourself only so much time in the game, never catching sight of the woman you'd married or your children at all.

And I remember how I survived the angry season, how I habitually wandered at the fall fairs that arrived like magic in the small towns just north of Toronto when I was old enough to leave the house for a few hours unnoticed. It was a kind of solace to look at the prizes awarded schoolchildren for drawings of pilgrims, at the winning pumpkin pies (imagining the mothers' faces floating benignly over their ready crusts), at the chickens and rabbits and steers in their pens, looking almost proud of their impending slaughter. And it used to cheer me up to throw balls at the clown with enormous floppy shoes, a red bulbous nose, and wet baggy trousers held up with suspenders, who fell into a large tub of water when someone throwing the baseball hit the target. It made me wonder why a grown man would do something so foolish — I used to tell myself he was probably somebody's father. And then I would throw the baseball, hitting the target more times than not, watching the man fall into the water with great antics of despair.

And it seems there was always a voice blaring from a loudspeaker, a platform beneath put up hurriedly, and if I turned quickly I would see families stopped in an unconscious huddle, staring blankly at some man in a tight suit chopping food or making dirt disappear with something invariably called a Superslicer or a Lintmaster. As a girl, I believed that a collection of gadgets held the families together as they watched, the children whining and pressing against their parents' legs, wanting sweets and a ride through the Tunnel of Horrors, the mothers and fathers conferring together about the thing being sold on that platform, the thing that would save them.

For years I went looking for inventions to keep people together.

And of course it was part of the ritual to fly high above the scene of squealing pigs and tawdry freak shows and press myself against the feeling of falling, screaming with a strange kind of abandon in the rush of air as the giant iron wheel swung up and around and down. For it had been there, on the ferris wheel, that there had sometimes seemed to be a last hope, something that might yet be the answer to your anger. But even then I knew I was gambling with a thing much scarcer than the chance of winning something at the covert booths where a man shouted, "Three shots for a quarter!", pulling money in his direction with a sly smile. And it was then I usually started to cry, the wheel seeming to drop down hard against my own life.

Eventually the wheel stopped, and the wash of fear and excitement in my stomach made me remember the feeling of dropping from that safe distance back to earth again. All the true things rushing back at me; the sharp air of autumn and the smell of roasting hot dogs rising from the small tents and the dust circling high above the pacers beating their hooves angrily into the summer-hard surface of the old dirt track. And the man at the bottom of the ride, who seemed to look the same each year, who always wiped his nose on his sleeve, hiked his bagging pants up into his groin sharply, pulled me out of my bobbing seat and put me on the ground again. In all the years he must have thought the thrill of the ride accounted for the wet streaks on my cheeks, my wild eyes.

And every year, it was true, I always felt more restless than content when I started toward home. I usually walked home the longest way possible so that I could look into the windows of the houses gathering their people for large dinners, the faces passing and joining and touching in the bright rectangles of light set against the dark.

So it seems I have long carried the angry season with me. Vati, you should know this about me — it happens every year in December. All at once everything seems changed. The days that have been passing almost without notice are suddenly a grim collection of gestures inordinately petty and cruel to others. And hopeless. The people I think I could love or have loved, even terrifyingly, seem sad and broken by the world, and not worthy of the slightest respect. The sounds and smells that shape life and hold it in place lose all their familiar attachments. Salt tastes like grass, my bare arm extended in the air feels like a shotgun with pale female skin and fine black hairs along the barrel. The sound of a child crying reminds me of its death many years down the road.

This year I found myself wanting to place blame for the desperate feeling with Dean. When I had my coffee in the mornings — Dean was, of course, rushing into the bedroom on his way out, bearing gifts, sweet gestures, knowing he could afford the caring then because he would soon have the space between us that would relieve him of me — I screamed at him of some damage he could not fathom. Then, terrified by my assault on him, I would say, "Here, feel my heart, it's beating too fast, it's always too fast." And then I would hear him leave and I would remain under the covers waiting for more sleep. Sleep that did not come. And I would simply lie there, feeling my pulse, telling myself I was too fragile a membrane, too thin and too brittle, to greet the things beyond my bed.

Sometimes I would laugh, because it all seemed so funny. Something is terribly wrong, I would admit in a whisper, although no one else was there to hear me. And then just as I might begin to think of the thing that was holding me down in the bed, stale and warm with my despair, I would doze. And have a jealous, restless sleep, which made me feel jumpy and still more angry on awakening.

I think you should know how I spent my days. I think you should know. For you, Vati, are responsible.

No matter when I woke up then, it seemed like that heavy thawing noon hour full of noise and motion I have always hated to enter unprepared. I would wake up feeling lost, feeling as old as the dust on my window ledges and as insubstantial as the light falling there. And then as heavy and dull as a woman still suspended in the worst moment of her childhood, still out of step with the world after all these years. Twenty-nine clumsy years. Thirty if you count the birthday Dean recently forgot.

Sometimes I was reminded of the strange pulsating feeling I had as a child when waking from chaotic dreams. I used to lie there, waiting innocently for an explanation, as though the dreams could be set right, or at least laid to rest. I would be caught up in the sensation of becoming alternately small and dry and lifeless, a speck of dust, and then growing huge elephant-like limbs in a bloated, overblown sense of blood and water and bone. I was always terrified of the feeling because I couldn't control the sensation at will.

And then I would look out my window and notice only that there was already so much snow and still an entire winter before me, and be numbed by the fact that there was nothing to do in the afternoon. And I would watch the neighbouring women all out with their children in the optimistic sunshine, greeting the mailman and dashing inside to answer their phones and outside again to the calls of their young ones and then here to place garbage pails and there to shovel bits of snow and I found that I hated them. Hated them, Vati.

And then I would cry endlessly, swearing I would never go outside in that cold, varnished air as long as they were all out Christmas shopping. All of them keen as knives to cut deep into their families with presents. While they flew from house to car to shops, arms full of the stocktaking that happens every year at this time, the forgiveness, the lies, the real loves. Instead I would remain inside the half-finished house (why do architects never finish their own houses?), which needed wallpaper and paint and had no plans whatsoever for the flaming of plum puddings or the guests drinking too much and leaning too close. I stayed here, and counted all the drops of water from my spilling taps, measuring the time spent watching afternoon movies on the black-and-white TV. I measured my pulse, my appetite, the pain in this throbbing headache, in that nerve below the left ovary, the coldness in one hand, the paleness of that cheek. So that when Dean arrived home late (always later than expected), I would have already measured everything of fragility in our home and in our being together.

What's wrong? he would repeat every day, looking briefly through the bathroom door where I was always in a condition of mild drunkenness, the bathwater as high as it could reach without drawing me under. The water good and hot. What's wrong? he would ask, his shoulders hunching in that way he has when he's angry. Damn him, I used to say. Why was he angry? I guess because he assumed I must have known why things seemed changed.

But one day, when he had already left, and he was no longer asking what was wrong, I smiled a little. I felt smug. That day I found a tiny bit of wrapping paper, the crinkly kind that we used at home when I was a child. It lay in the last pages of a book I hadn't opened for years, beside a bookmark made of dried flowers. Flowers that grew in Europe forty years ago. And then it happened that I looked absentmindedly at the calendar I hadn't otherwise stopped to consider for weeks. After that it seemed that I heard the date mentioned out loud again and again, from one small mocking voice on the radio, in the muffled greetings of the neighbours who were entering and leaving their houses . . . even the black-and-white faces caught in the plot of the afternoon movie seemed to speak only of this day in December.

"It's December the fifth," I would have said to Dean, had he walked in the door. That's what I would have said as an explanation had he once again asked what was wrong.

It's incredible how that date conjures up the feeling of great white spaces where something has happened and been forgotten, as in a fresh covering of snow over last year's gardens and things left undone. I play a kind of game with this memory, for this is what I finally realized it to be, moving deliberately around the house, making lists of all the books that have never been read in our shelves, or rooting around in the kitchen drawers for something small that seems out of place. It's as though I'm reassuring myself that the things of the past no longer have a bearing. The silver finally gleams in its right place in the drawer, forks just so, knives looking kinder, and the books are all arranged alphabetically once more. I stand still, looking with obstinate calm at the sunlight glancing off the icicles outside my windows. How many years ago now? Fifteen? Twenty?

And I will recover. As in all the other years, the dreams of you cutting us all to pieces, running your family one by one through your Skilsaw, the blood running into the old porous surfaces of workbench and wooden floor, and myself being the helpless — am I helpless? — witness, will dissolve into foggy nights of heavy sleep. And I will begin to feel closer once again to the people and things that hold some comfort. The world will become once again necessary to me.

It's true; by Christmas, all that usually remains is a slim gesture or two mocking the past. Like the way I still catch myself watching how far my wrists lie on the table top when I'm eating. My hands still shake when they reach the place where you would have counted them a fault in manners, brushing them angrily into my lap. That's the kind of small reminder that stays with me; I will probably always see the red marks in the shape of a man's hand where you pressed so hard for the love you wanted.

So it seems I'm still angry with you underneath. That's what it is, then.

I can still recall Mutti asking carefully how you would get the four-seater plane out of the basement without leaving the profiles of wings in the house she loved. (Your latest dream, you had assured us, was quite safe. We would simply spend more time together as a family defying gravity, floating freely in the sky. My father the pilot. The terrifying expanse of sky holding us close together.)

You had laughed curtly, looking down at your plate, your jaws chewing, your cheeks drawn in tight with the effort of the answer. You had said then, between bites, "I'll tear down the new extension on the house." You had thrown down your knife and fork with a clatter then and tilted your head back, roaring so that your Adam's apple went up and down like a piston. Knowing that your laughter was law. Looking to your children for approval as you began singing a lusty song of camaraderie you had either just invented or else carried with you since your days as a paratrooper. The refrain made us all join you in laughing until we were crying. I think it was just because the word *Flugzeuge*, drawn out in your poor singing, sounded so out of place.

And I suppose the ludicrous image of a house falling down and a plane flying off into the blue with our father inside appealed to us. I suppose we thought you wonderful. You always possessed more weight in our minds than Mutti's careful love for a house in continual stages of renovation, her gardens creeping cautiously to the boundaries of your energies. We didn't even stop to think of her convictions of time and space. Weren't we all living just to please you, after all? We never thought about that then, how that might be wrong. We just lived it amorphously, like the vague shapes in someone else's imagination. In your imagination.

So it seems clear I would be angry when I think of what you did to my mother, to us all. I can hear my voice almost shouting, like a defiant child's, whenever I speak of you, even yet. When I think about it, my slight lisp probably started in those slow afternoons of the old radio shows when I used to sit on your lap, mimicking the overly dramatic voices with you while you tried to improve your English. Whenever I think of you I still get that feeling of having to sit too still, hearing your uneven syllables against the background of the eerie music, your knees getting harder and harder. And yet I smile when I remember that.

Of course my memory of you does not begin at the beginning. There are stories passed on, however, from those who saw you then, just newly arrived from the old country, penniless, as you so often pointed out to your children for the effect it might create.

I suppose most of the stories must have been my mother's. She would have known best about those things. Her stories seemed to protect me from the cruel event that was later to end them. Her stories kept you intact, at the centre of things, never quite real, out of reach of judgment or blame.

But there were also stories that seemed to predict what would happen and even take some sort of satisfaction in the outcome. They were stories told by the others. I could sense what they knew of you — to them, you gave the impression of being tall because you stood very erect, had hard grey eyes that narrowed easily, as though in response to some inner command, liked order in your home and obedience in your family. Admired loyalty in your friends, had few friends. To them you were anxious to achieve the greater things in life; the small victories of your wife, your children and friends, scarcely interested you. You were known to have clicked your heels in public and to have made a joke out of that gesture, expecting others to understand. The others could sense that you would not be crossed in any way, that you were brutally unforgiving at disappointments. That you were continually disappointed.

I grew up in the stories, their stories, her stories. And I have taken what I can remember from the way my mother spoke of you and from what little the others outside our family knew, and I have tried to find you.

Once before I was even born, Mutti had packed Käthe, then four, on her back and had left her home in the small German town on the Rhine. She must have left in a hurry, in fact she didn't even have enough money with her to buy Käthe a fruit drink on the way (she'd walked twelve miles on a windy, rainy day), and had arrived at Oma's house without any explanation. And without any plans for the future. Although Oma never asked.

Oma is very good at this story. And at the accompanying guilt. Sometimes I think I go to Germany every few years just to see whether the story's changed, or whether the guilt has been lifted from her small, careworn shoulders. She's had several strokes now, so her voice shifts in the telling and the story's shorter, although the main things remain. "I never liked your father." That's the way she begins.

"Three times, three times I walked to the post office with the letter of consent for your mother to marry him. I was the head of the household then, with your grandfather gone. Somewhere dead in Russia. And three times I walked back home again without mailing it." Oma's arms are shaky when they lift the letter three times to the imagined mailbox and then fall, letting her hands drop again.

"But she said she loved him and it was wartime (here the small, quiet woman who was imprisoned several times during the war for refusing to say 'Heil Hitler' raises a trembling arm in mock salute to the *Führer* long gone), so I finally sent it. Although I said to myself, this thing will be no good, this marriage.

"And here your mother came, almost five years later, with the daughter he later disowned on her back, and you perhaps already in her womb, and I knew even then she was thinking of her self-respect. And also of her pride. And how hard it must have been for her to say nothing.

"She stayed a few days with me, looking nervous and eating practically nothing, although Käthe seemed in good humour and wanted to stay forever. Yes, that's what your sister said. And one day your father telephoned and your mother cried then and went back to him. Back to her marriage, thinking everything would be different. Your father had such a way of talking to her, making her believe anything. Not long after, he must have talked to her of Canada, for they moved far away from me. So far away."

It must torment Oma still that she found her daughter during the war, only to lose her once again. Already then, she couldn't shake the feeling that she was permitting a kind of intimacy that would somehow lead to dying.

Women feel the guilt more readily, I think. As though there's a part in our anatomies that's made especially for the hiding and bringing forth of guilt. And this capacity for guilt, I think it runs in families, from woman to woman, like the childbearing troubles they inherit or the way their lips purse or their eyes shut out the truth.

Take your mother, for example. She had a certain amount to be guilty for, for all her beauty and trappings. People say I look like her, although she was fuller-faced, softer-featured. No doubt I have inherited the thing that made her look solemn in so many photos, her dark side. When the Russians were moving west and driving all the people out of what is now Poland, across the Vistula, Klara — known as the beautiful complainer — came to live with Mutti's family. Perhaps you never heard this story. Or perhaps you somehow forgot it.

But I hear that when she arrived, bringing her trunks and hatboxes and favourite trinkets, she was moving in an earlier spirit, not the spare and simultaneously generous spirit of wartime. And then when the Russians were again on the doorstep, the tanks rolling over the small schoolhouse in the Prussian village, Klara took the whole thing personally, as though this were some sort of bad luck visited only, or at least especially, upon her. So when the hot rustle of crop burning and raping began, there she sat, a woman proud of the fact she'd never let her husband see her naked, proud of her once clean house left behind and her clocks never running down, there she sat weeping for the things that would soon be lost to her. While the other women were packing potatoes and putting on several layers of underwear, Klara cried out, "Oh, my laces, my laces," and sobbed about the family silver.

She rubbed her hands together, the dry skin showering off like flakes of snow, and tried to put all her jewelry on. The other women took it off again while Klara struggled; a sparkling sapphire ring or a gold necklace was an invitation to disaster. There Klara almost died, amid the gunfire and the fires of the small homes burning to the ground. "You could almost smell the rape of the young girls and grandmothers," Oma always says at this point in the story. "Here were the Russian soldiers who hadn't changed their clothes in months, bending over the young and old alike, and here was Klara, refusing to move."

They all tried in vain to reason with her, all the aunts and cousins now dead, and Oma, too. "This is life we are fighting for, not the necklaces and brooches, not the sparkle and the glitter. Simply life. Get up, Klara, get up. We must go. We must save the thing you cannot see, the thing of blood and nerves."

She wept so bitterly, obviously giving up to the fear within, that they decided to find her a safe haven with a family in Treustock. And in all the commotion of finding a refuge for Klara, people were separated, people who should have never been apart. Mutti and her mother.

To separate people is a dangerous thing; nothing speaks of it so clearly as the story of Mutti in those eight months she was caught between fronts. Cut off on one side from her mother and sister, and on the other from you, her young husband. Oma told me this story, so it has a ring of admiration about it that Mutti would never have acknowledged or fashioned for herself. For it was Mutti who saved Klara's life, and it was Mutti who was then left behind. So I see my mother shine in this story, where she would, in her own telling of it, simply have passed quietly through events.

Oma is hiding with others in a barn — how many people are sheltered there, moving stealthily, using light and water and sleep like precious gifts, moving furtively in the stench of the straw and the darkness of the old barn, I don't know. But one day on the radio transmitter they have set up, a message comes for Hardmute, Mutti's maiden name. Is there anyone here named Hardmute? Oma rises from her place in the dark in a dress I imagine to be maroon or dark brown, fearing the worst (for I suppose one had equal hopes and fears when answering this kind of call), then hears the voice of her Charlotte on the radio, hears the daughter's voice she's long thought to be dead or lost. "My Charlotte," she cries into the receiver. "Yes, yes. On the train. *Sei aber vorsichtig, mein Kind.*"

There would be a train — not many were running in those last days of the war — and the train would be passing right by that barn just east of this town and south of the burned-down church, and there in the corn fields the Hardmute women would wait for her. Wait for my mother.

They wait all day, for several days. On the third evening, as the last rays of the sun are glancing off the rails of the track (or so they imagine, for the rails have long been rusty from lack of use), my aunt Hanna can feel the iron tremble. She lies there with her head to the ground, as she's waited for days, and cries out, *"Ein Zug, Mutti! Ein Zug!"* Soon it comes into view, a black, ominous chain of coal cars moving slowly up the track.

They look up, they have never looked so hard, Oma's eyes still sharp as a bird's, Hanna, who was short-sighted even as a child, blinking back the tears. And there, sitting on top of the second coal car, a young woman with blonde hair shining — how could her hair be shining through all the years of the war? — her hair shining, and her arms waving and waving. And she sees them, her sister and mother who are shouting and crying out her name — Charlotte! Charlotte! — and my mother, she rides like a queen in a procession held in her honour, her blonde hair shining as she rides the sooty black coal car. And one, two, three and off she jumps, into the tender shoots of corn, the three rolling on the ground and embracing forever and ever, finding all the joy that's been removed in the long years of war. The sun sets and the women lie on the wet earth in the corn field, the young stalks waving and waggling as the bodies laugh and hold each other and laugh again.

An urgent message the next day; that the train has stopped further on down the line at such and such a place and that there is room for some to move west. There is room for those who want to chance the journey, rather than wait in the barn, without moving. But many would never make it from the train to a safe place; many would die in their own urine and from the heartbreak of a journey that would seem endless and end only too quickly and too hard.

But these three women in my family, they catch the train, and they stand close together, their feet wet in the filth, their backs swaying against one another. They haven't stopped holding each other since the corn field. They are no longer separate, and that is the main thing. They sing songs and tell stories of when the sisters were young girls, and some of the others around them listen and seem to want to smile.

Then there is a loud explosion. Half the train car is left on the tracks and the other half rises into the air along with the legs and arms and voices that have somehow left their bodies. But there in the rear half of the car, like a miracle, as Oma always says in this part of the story, are the three still standing together. Bombs are falling somewhere in the farmlands nearby, and then someone comes by the train shouting, "The war is over! The war is over!"

The three laugh; isn't it funny the bombs should still be falling at war's end. Perhaps peace will be just another form of war. But they leave the broken shell of the train, and for a moment the three women can imagine something better than the dead and the dying all around them.

And all at once, Mutti, perhaps thinking of this better time and place, reaches for a small sack she's carried, bound to her underclothes around her waist. A sack she's carried through all the years of the war. And when she finds her dress has torn and the sack is nowhere there, she cries out, "The war is over and I have lost my shoes, my silver shoes."

"Was machst du, Charlotte? Was ist los, mein Kind?"

The three look between the dying and the dead; then suddenly there is one of the slippers, the moon beaming on it, and there is the other, next to a quiet-faced child in the field. And she puts on her shoes at the end of the war, her silver dancing shoes, and dances a slow, painful dance of love for those who have made it through and are still together. The moon shines on her pale arms raised high in celebration.

The last gestures of war somehow remained; while my mother held her arms high in the hope of things being better long after that dance in a distant landscape of war, I see you, your whole life long, as a man still wearing the civilian clothes he'd stolen from a clothesline somewhere near Raum, with his arms raised so the American soldiers could check for SS marks. A man ashamed and confused at war's end by this gesture of giving up. A man cannot hold his arms that way forever without growing weary. Suddenly, on the day the war ended, everything you'd been led to believe as a boy — you were only eleven when Hitler came to power, only seventeen when you joined the army — suddenly everything was again possible, and nothing could be said for certain to be right. When you felt the greatest uncertainty — that's when you came to Canada.

Right from the first, Canada must have been synonymous with defeat for you — the Americans had denied you entrance into the States — as though in this country it would be hard to ever be anything but just beginning. You and your beautiful young wife arrived in Canada penniless — that is the story you have told again and again — and spent a first grim year in a basement apartment in a house on Madison

Avenue near Bloor, where I was born. Where I was to end up years later, making noises of angst and anti-establishment during my university days. But you were a dreamer and you and Mutti would prowl around Toronto on Sunday afternoons when you were released from the confines of your government job and imagine where you would live, what material pleasures were finally your due, how everything would look in a few years' time.

My mother would have been content with a house of any shape with a garden and a place for the children. A porch with a swing would have been an extra-special treat. She had few demands to make. But you, you wanted land, and you wanted room for workshops and swimming pools and attached office space. Some days you wished for a farm, in other moments you wanted to live by the water; then a houseboat would have been fine. And sometimes you wanted it all, the water, the farm with the animals and pastures and the distance, the warmth of an old house with every modern gadget within. You wanted to breed dogs, rebuild cars, harvest your own crops, kayak across a body of water you could say was yours alone — you grew restless on the Sunday drives, moving in ever-widening circles of expectation. And you made your intentions clear, talking to farmers, boat builders, real-estate entrepreneurs, schoolteachers, churchgoers. People were aware of the things you wanted. And some did not like you for your desire, which seemed so inappropriate to a country with so much to give. And others found you hard to like because they could feel the damnation that went with the desire, they could feel what would happen if you never reached your goals.

Uncle (so named because we, as children, had no uncles) and Lily have told me of the first time they set eyes on you. They had straightened up from their steamy garden on a humid Toronto afternoon in late summer and seen what looked like a lonesome man, woman, and child. But oddly bound, somehow, as though they belonged together. They had seen a young mother, late in her second pregnancy, and a girl of about five tagging unwillingly along the dry hedges of their street in Scarborough. And you were there, the upright young husband, guiding their weariness fiercely along the blistering sidewalks. You were seeing to it, with your eyes, that there would be land you could claim to inhabit, together, as a family, in the open and almost uninhabited country called Canada.

You had leaned toward the couple quietly gardening and had shouted, "Is there any land for sale in this area?" Your syllables were stark and uneven, but your English was good for a newcomer. Uncle, squatting in the sun, scraping the earth from a carrot in his hands, replied slowly that the Veteran's Land Act governed most of the lots. That's how they'd managed to acquire theirs, he said. You stiffened, laughing harshly, extending a scarred knee beneath your khaki shorts — "A New Zealand bullet. Wrong type of veteran, I suppose." Your German accent broke through unmistakably then.

The couple put down their gardening tools then, Lily serving an icy pitcher of lemonade in the cool, dark house as a kind of open-handedness to your uneasy defence.

The fact is that Uncle and Lily were two of the most decent people you could have shouted at in the early years in Canada. For them there had been no war great enough to separate the gruff German on that sidewalk from any other human being. And perhaps Uncle had felt a certain sense of adventure, perhaps even danger, in meeting you on Scarborough soil late in the summer of 1952. The year I was born.

I've been told we literally marched into their gentle gardening scene. For when Uncle had made some fine remarks about the older things in life continuing, you apparently stood up from your chair, put down your lemonade with a wry smile, and proceeded to click your heels together. Mutti blushed and pulled at your sleeve to stop you, but Uncle simply remarked, as though he were merely curious, and not an equal and opposite survivor of the last war, as though he were Nick Carraway dealing with the Gatsby he had long awaited with the calm of a high-school principal, "That's very nice. Show me how you do that."

Then, Uncle has said, the two of you went back and forth across the thick carpet clicking your heels together, and laughing. You talked together that day for hours, the women looking on in some disbelief; Uncle speaking in a slow, measured way broken by his deep, joyful laugh, you forcing your words out like fists in the sweet, lazy summer you could scarcely accept. Uncle, several generations Canadian, ten years older than you were, steady in his eyes, and you, the young father, fearful, gauging every word, ashamed of the pride you still carried in your heels pressing together hard like that.

The two women were also to become profound friends, although they must have envied the almost childish abandon the two men shared. That first day, as you gathered your family suddenly, abruptly, wondering if you'd said too much, Uncle suggested you return the following Sunday for a traditional Canadian dinner. The invitation was accepted, but you had the final word. You said you doubted whether Canadians had traditions, at least ones they could admit to on a Sunday. Poor Mutti, large-bellied, had tugged once more at your sleeve, protesting. Perhaps already on my behalf.

Soon a sparsely furnished house, with plenty of room for your vision and Mutti's gardens, sat uncertainly on the bare soil near the Humber River. But even with your new-found land, four acres with a bush, a swamp, a hill, and a solitary brown house with few neighbours, you were still searching in large circles for things yet unfulfilled in the dream. The windows of your house lacked curtains, the wooden floors lay cold and bare in the mornings, there was always a feeling of looking outward, beyond the birch trees, beyond the garage, to something yet missing.

Some Sundays Lily and Uncle made brave forays into our rough territory to help you find that missing thing; you were always moving walls, making furniture — they sat calmly by, handing you tools, drinking Mutti's coffee.

And on alternate weekends our family settled longingly, as though into a womb, into Sundays with Lily and Uncle, wood-panelled Sundays, gleaming with moments of silver and sparkling glass, soft music and sweet arguments going on far into the night. Those Sundays were a respite from the struggle; as children, we grew to have favourite window seats and leather chairs, favourite desserts, favourite smells of roast meat and flowers in the vases, which were as much a feeling of home as our own, more exposed existence.

In Uncle and Lily's house, life had settled and was all there, complete. It was a comfort to move between the cherrywood and fruitwood tables with elegant, spidery legs, smelling the sap of the logs in the fireplace and the rich scent of their books. I would savour the moment of switching on the lamp with the shade of pressed wild flowers and picking up a thick, leather-bound volume of bird song or a novel of the last century. The evenings would grow late, you were content for the moment with Uncle, and I would read accounts of muddy York and the Plains of Abraham as though my own family were somehow moving through that history. Safe and warm by the fire, I could imagine the early dangers of settlement in the strange land called Canada.

And oh, how I remember the dinners, large helpings of pumpkin pie or trifle in the candlelight, Lily's small trembling voice asking, "How much?" and her kind hands giving more. But my favourite time was when the voices of the two men would begin to rise. The logs would crackle, I would pretend to sleep behind a huge volume of fairy tales and then it would happen. Uncle's silver head and your jet-black silhouette would lean together, your faces animated, joined together in some spirited argument, usually about politics or education. In spite of your eagerness to prove your points, the disagreements were never bitter, and ended with Uncle touching his friend on the shoulder and saying, "Well, it's getting late."

You would drive home peacefully — I would watch you from the back seat. And under the passing streetlights you would suddenly seem my father.

The history of muddy York I have almost forgotten now, but I learned by heart the arguments of men. If the men began before supper, the ritual required that the women retreat into the small, steamy kitchen complete with a dachshund that rarely moved from under the small breakfast table. There they would trade the secrets of their passage through the rising and falling of hems and bittersweet mothering. The children ran back and forth through the swinging door, upturning chairs to make cars, or sifting through Lily's messy drawer, the one that held bits of string and rubber bands and all the ingredients for making things. The two women gently toppled the hierarchy of their husbands with their discourse of flower beds and children's beds and their own marriage beds. But I could sense that it was somehow natural for women to have this bond and that one could learn their kind of talking by clearing the table after dinner or listening from time to time through that swinging door. But even as a young girl I understood that the heated, almost angry way the men carried on was what I was after. That it was a privilege to hear them. It was a rare and generous thing for you and Uncle to break the otherwise solitary circles of men in that time. And laugh so hard, and sometimes even weep a little.

It was especially rare because it surmounted your theory of wariness. Even since your years in the army, it had been your habit to decide right from the beginning of knowing someone, right from the first words spoken, how they would act in the event of war. Of course you never told anyone that; I just knew how that must have seemed a practical and necessary consideration. To decide who would raise his arm first to strike, who would say nothing (even under torture), who would cry out to protect himself, who would call out to save the others. Who would take up new clothes from a stranger's washing to begin again, raising both arms in surrender, looking the long-fought enemy straight in the eye. Who could leave the harm of war behind, and who would always remember it. For you believed that the worst had already happened. I heard you say that once to Uncle.

And that realization did not offer you much solace. Instead, you carried the dead weight of the thing named "the worst" with you. And some days it pulled you down.

When I was still too young to know of gas chambers and mass graves and Hitler's acts of cowardice, I used to close my eyes and try to imagine the terrible things you must have seen in the war. I didn't have much to go on, for you didn't talk of the war as a series of events, but only as this intangible feeling of warning about the worst thing that could happen. And the worst I could come up with always seemed to involve our own family; I would picture you holding your own wife and children prisoner, keeping us awake long past our bedtimes and asking us questions we couldn't answer, I would see you torturing my brother Martin with cold water or fire, and the worst was always when you forced my mother to make a choice between two equally horrible things. The choice always involved the children and a shallow grave behind the house that was marked the same way as the grave in which our dog had been buried, with a bent stick and a rock the size of a human head. That was the worst, and it hadn't happened yet. And I thought, as a very young child, that it never would. So I didn't altogether understand your fears. But I know you had decided on the day you met Uncle, perhaps while you were both clicking your heels together and laughing, that Uncle could be trusted. That Uncle and Lily had no part in any of the world's worst things.

For some it may have been different. But for us, for the people who lived with the man the neighbourhood knew as the German, the war was never really over. It was still going on in our heads whenever butter was spread thinly, too thinly (I always wanted more butter) over the bread. As children we were constantly reminded how our parents had lined up for days and nights for mottled potatoes while the smell of rotting meat, meat that would never be handed out, stayed with them long after they went home hungry. "We stood like animals, hoping for one potato, one spoon of butter," you would roar at suppertimes. "And now the children we starved for never have enough," you would add lamely, not knowing yourself how things fit together. And then your children would go out and scream with zeal in some twilight and we would remember the war all over again from that sound.

And so it went from the butter to the sound to the lull of sleeping when we would think it was finally quiet. And safe. But suddenly the memory of cold metal and the snap of light passing over dark faces, the snap of locks and keys and guns and barbed wire on bone, the snap of false accusation and true guilt, would visit in our dreams, even in the children's faces, as we reared from our pillows and asked in hollow voices, "Who's there?" The sound was always the same, the sound that woke us, a cold, metallic snap of necks broken and children gutted, and mothers lying to defend their young, and the raping of the women lying . . . the sound was always a snap.

The sound was a snap, even in broad daylight, although I think my mother had the gift to forget the sound and hear the rest of the immense universe. To forget. A gift you never forgave her for.

She could forget in a solemn hour of kneeling by her flower beds, pressing the black dirt with her long fingers, or she could forget in a brief moment of badminton on a summer's day. Sometimes the cone-shaped white bird would fly high above the morning glories and the sunflowers, soaring far beyond the sagging net strung between veranda and garage. And then her tightly strung body, still sharp and pure in outline (even after three children), would forget the way things were supposed to be. And she would flirt with the air, she would laugh at some sweep of her wrist that cut clean from family and friends and everything known, and she would float free.

And you would see, the German would see. And your cheeks would hollow and your eyes grow narrow. You would see what was happening, the children all joining in this moment of freedom, their bodies promising loyalties to moments in the air, without memory or knowing. And you would bring us all down, all together, our heads bowed, our eyes still sparkling, our mouths tilted with laughter. You would bring us down with the memory of that sound, with the snap. And we would see how important it was, and we would go with your solemn message into some colder, darker place, which continued without stopping from the past. Which lay across our beds in the morning like a deep shadow and was not so easy to forgive in you as simply to live with. And it was only in certain moments that we began to see how living with that sound, with the snap, was a kind of punishment. We were caught in some place just short of war's end.

I suppose that we, as children, and Mutti, were on the same side with you in the war. In a great number of battles we were never quite sure who the enemy was. For the longest time I think we believed, along with you, that we would somehow win whatever it is one wins in a war. We had always done everything together. Often we had played games, five pairs of hands shuffling cards, throwing dice; there were long silences, nervous staccato laughter pattered in the room at intervals. There were arguments, your voice whistling through the house, my mother's hands running over one another anxiously. But still it was acknowledged by the way doors closed, voices hushed, the way we all suffered, connected along the same ribbon of pain in our dreams, that we were still together. That we would play games again, gambling and losing.

We even had a career together. Unusual for a family. And you were proud of that. Proud, yet anguished by your wife's hands drawing perfectly straight lines along the T-squares while you paced a worn path in the old carpet in your study. She was the all-too-beautiful draftsman you had inherited along with a wife and mother of your brood; after all, she had almost as much schooling in architecture as you did. That's where you'd met, at the university in Hanover; you took leaves from the front to continue your education and then you would depart for months to God knows what fate. Even then she had completed your drawings, completed your picture of how things should look. You had always returned, angry with war, to look over her shoulder.

And even after you'd been in Canada some years, whenever you saw that slim, golden-haired woman leaning over the sloping tables, you remembered the war, and you felt something fragile and open about your career. It often seemed to you that she was dreaming beyond the straight lines, that she was smiling soft circles when she should have known how important it was for you to win the competitions, stay ahead of the rest who'd had all the opportunities, prove something to those who all somehow belonged in this godforsaken country more than you. And perhaps that's what it was, this feeling that she belonged in Canada, that she was happy here. She should have cared more for the straight lines, but she was dreaming of her children and her flowers in the garden. And sometimes when she felt you looking at her, and she looked up from the transparent paper, startled, you felt she was dreaming of her own life. Something hiddden from you.

You were best at designing when the three children were quiet, almost as though they didn't exist, when your only draftsman — the woman you'd married — was afraid and drew her lines more sharply. That's when the buildings took shape, at the last moment, when you were angry, your mouth a thin, set line, your arms and legs and cheeks and chin all angles that could be measured by their respective tensions. And you were always furious the nights before the lines had to become finished city halls or art galleries or churches. The house would smell of ammonia then, and the blueprint machine would whir and cast eerie slits of light across the room and out into the hall.

There was order in those lines, which you relied on. And order in your winning. And yet to win the competitions was a great struggle, and sometimes a great concession. You paid dearly in having the chance to finally erect the buildings, let your ideas stand on their own — for there were always people who saw the buildings as less than you knew them to be, as cornerstones to their religion or local politics. They often failed to see the miracle in the slabs of mortar, long beams arching over congregations. They could see only how much the walls of block glass would cost, how the depths and lengths and heights of the structures meant to inspire the spirit would set budgets back. You would get shortness of breath when this happened; fights with contractors punctuated your days, your nights were long with pacing. In the mornings we would see a path worn into the carpet like the pattern a race horse leaves in his stall, or a caged animal makes in his small space. And like the race horse or the tiger, you were thinking only of how not to give in. How not to compromise the best line in a year's worth of design, how not to relinquish the hold on your buildings.

Your buildings? They were simple enough, and honest, deploring any sort of kitsch or sentimentality. In that sense they were timeless structures, not trapped by fashion or the fate of the era in which they rose. But they were probably old-fashioned in one sense: although the shapes were clean and modern, with lines converging and pulling apart again in bold forms suggesting freedom, in reality you were concerned with holding people together. Unlike many other designs of the time, leaving much to chaos and accidental interpretation, being more playful in scope, leading to endless arguments about the function of structures, your buildings were serious. There was always a message or a moral to your entranceway or second storey. They seemed to be embodiments to a morality you'd carried with you since your days as a paratrooper in the war. (Once I'd heard you say that war consisted of floating down unnoticed into the quiet of the mountains in Crete, and reading your schoolbooks in peace. In peace, you'd said. Had you dreamed of church spires with gunfire in the background, or children in sun-filled modern classrooms after war's end? Somehow I believed you had.) Your buildings were the glass and concrete forms of something rigid and unbending within, something shaped in the bloody days of your early manhood. Something that could protect the fragile human spirit.

So it was easy to see then why others' opinions, their lack of imagination about a portico or a skylight, served to wound you. You wore your buildings like a protective skin, allowing in light here and there, keeping in warmth, holding the hopeful sound of human voices, and whenever doorways were changed or roofs altered to slant west, rather than east, the change inflicted an injury. The designs that were denied existence you carried stillborn within, and the compromises you wore as raw and open sores forever left exposed to wind and sun and the Canadian winter.

Once I had a dream of you standing like a giant on the hill next to our house and wearing your buildings like a suit of armour, layered for protection, and ornamented to uphold your honour. I think there was a hierarchy in the way I imagined it: the factories you wore like sturdy boots and leggings, the offices and government buildings you hung around your waist, the schools you flung over your back and carried lightly like one of the rucksacks you'd carried as a youth to your father's country school, and your churches, why, they rose from your shoulders like wings, and were a shining crown upon your head. In the dream you grew taller and taller, the churches seemed to reach the sky, and then the hill stood bare once more.

Perhaps the Lutheran church in the small community north of Toronto was your first real victory. For years of Sundays you faced the northern wall made entirely of glass, looking beyond the black-robed pastor speaking of God, and wished for more of the feeling you'd inherited with this building. Not knowing whether it was a religious awe or one of the greatest sins of man, pride. You had to admit you had designed the wide wooden pews for those who had already abandoned their guilt, and the way light fell on the shoulders of those lined up for communion made them seem already forgiven by a power greater than themselves. During the sermons you watched over your flock carefully to see that none of your spotless, handsomely dressed children would wiggle or whisper, and you noted with satisfaction how the glass wall drew their attention as much as the message or the hymns. When the pastor intoned "bringing sinners back to the fold" or "lightening our Christian loads," the children would look beyond the pulpit to the ravine filled with squirrels and raccoons, to the tall bird-ridden evergreens. Your wife sang hymns in a trembling voice and looked happy beside you and all the eyes of the congregation seemed fixed on the immense window beyond the pulpit, on the light changing there, the clouds reforming, the snow falling.

You were a man who rarely bowed his head, but you became strangely reverent during the closing prayer, when the minister would often offer thanks for the lovely place of worship they enjoyed. Then you would remember the day they'd asked one of their own, a fellow worshipper, a German, to design their new church. The new church was a far cry from the days of crowded worship in the old parsonage, some standing outside on the grass, even in rain or sleet, mouthing the words of the service bravely. The new church was a victory for the congregation.

So for ten years you went to worship on Sunday mornings, the congregation greeting you as a hero in the tall, glorious structure you had given them even before you'd passed your Canadian examinations in architecture. That church became a symbol for you, the plainness of the brick walls, the generous wooden pews, the tall and elegant cross of suffering that reared up thirty feet at the front of the church, before the glass wall. There, beneath the cloudlike white lamps suspended from the high ceiling, there, small and merely human before the radiant glass wall, because you felt safe, you exalted in the feeling of loosening, of letting go.

But gradually the scene of seasons' change and morning light behind the glass wall began to change. The once-green ravine crowned with sky became littered with the tiled roofs of new houses, all neat in rows between the fewer poplars and firs. And gradually, as the glass wall was darkened, so the faces around you, once private and proud, changed as well, and seemed restless, transparent. The others had slowly lost their common sense of displacement from their homelands, their need for one another, and when the hush fell over the congregation and the sermons started, a young, red-faced Canadian minister leading them all to and from pain and redemption, well . . . gradually you felt them become separate persons at worship. Only joined for the moment. Almost a decade after the earlier hard-won dollars fell from the tight fists into the offering plates, the money was easy-flowing and the faces constantly shifting, unsettled. Full of a new kind of freedom. The others were no longer joined by necessity and struggle. Their only guilt was one now before God, a fleeting, forgivable guilt seen only on Sundays — you could see that. The others wore casual clothes now, often came without their children, and had relaxed that posture of leaning forward so common to people afraid of failure.

When they stood in groups by the front doors after the service, blinking in the sunshine, they often laughed at their earlier hardships those years back. The new church, with the glass wall and the formidable cross of salvation, became less of a miracle, and it was plain to see they believed their struggle to be over.

For you it was never over. In your pew there were still five pairs of hands clasped in prayer, five who were always together. When you looked at the bowed heads of your family, their hair shining in the light of the candles passed down the pews at Christmas — and it was soon only at Christmas that you came to the church — you could see their struggle would never be finished. And that's what finally made them different.

You resisted the truth as long as you could. But one day when you chanced to look at your children and they looked back at you, directly, questions in their eyes, one day when you heard your wife singing with a bold sound that had once been secret and meek, one day when you thought you could see the changes even in your own family, then you decided to lead them away from the danger. They would still dress well on Sundays, think of God somewhat; but instead of taking the car from the garage, they would gather round you and read passages from *The Family Altar*, take long walks together by the river, sing songs around the piano, and leave the churchgoing to the others. That day you made up your mind, and they simply stopped going to the church you had built. And all that you had dreamed of in the generous pews was soon to be forgotten, or remembered only bitterly. In your eyes the family had no place to go but deep within their own small circle to survive.

Oh yes, you recognized the threat of your early success; once it had seemed you would never have enough food, have land of your own, dress in anything but the heavy, shapeless clothes of the past. But suddenly you had several cars in the driveway, and money came in lump sums greater than you had ever imagined and only made you wish for more. And your children were suddenly growing up; they were not so easily led, tugging in separate directions away from home. But your wife made you the most fearful; when you looked at her you could see she was blooming. After all the years of hardship, washing diapers by hand, dividing the food for the children first, her eyes shadowed with weariness, she was thriving in her new life. And unlike the uncertain years of your courtship in the war, and your first years of marriage fraught with worry, she was no longer looking only to you for her joy; she was swelling with the growth of her children, with new-found friends, with moments you no longer shared. And so perhaps because of her more than anything, because of your wife, you wanted to start at the beginning again.

You suddenly remembered with longing the bitterness and beauty of those first years. The first bottle of wine, the first baby pram, the first fur coat for your wife. Your first camera, recording your survival. Everything came to be compared with the feeling of first coming to Canada; your conversations were filled with old wooden trunks and faded red feather beds you had brought on the ocean voyage, with the German classical books and the artifacts of war, your medals and the pictures of your colleagues, fellow students — row upon row of those who had not survived — and you seemed to savour the lost feeling of having no money, no family waiting on the new continent, nothing except your wife, younger then, and your eldest daughter, holding a hand from each parent.

You remembered the house. You had discovered it in a squalid yard littered with debris on a Sunday drive to Peterborough. And you had brought it back in two halves on large floats, the dark-shingled walls split down the middle, the neighbours standing open-mouthed, amazed at the German's will. And you had set the house on blocks on the several acres near the Humber River just about the time Hurricane Hazel had threatened the family once more. You had imagined the worst as the winds and the rains swept the roofs off the older cottages near the river — the Lutheran pastor let you stay in the parsonage — but the storm had passed you by, leaving the barely settled house standing on a slight rise sparsely knit with grass. In the year that followed, you and your young wife planted young poplars and small weeping willows supported by sticks, and the yellow clusters of marsh marigolds bloomed in the swamp behind the house, among the trunks of the white birches. You had worked harder than you could imagine now, your wife peeling off the blistering paint and carrying heavy wheelbarrow loads of sand and rocks. You remembered her pale shins, constantly bruised, and the way she continued, even when she'd broken several small bones in her left foot.

You kept a photo of your wife in those years in your wallet; she was holding your second daughter — I was just born — in a cardboard box, standing on the planks around the footings of the house. Your wife seemed, and probably was, innocent. And she was very pretty, wearing a dress you remembered well, full of dark, rich colours, and laced up at the bodice. Of course the photo was in black and white. There was a wheelbarrow tipped on its side and a huge, dark hole in front of her. But her smile seemed to say there was no danger, only future, in that hole.

Over the years her smiles, which had once been either sad or sweet, were harder to read, and the house was never completed. Oh, it was joined in the middle and was gradually painted, dark brown shingles and ochre window ledges. I was already ten, no longer the baby in the box, when I was asked to paint all the mullioned windows one summer holiday. I worked on the project from the time school ended to the day it began once more in the fall, moving the ladder slowly around the circumference of the house. For two months I was angry because I heard the other children on the street playing carefree games while I painted. But there was never any question of complaining or quitting the job before it was done; I was careful to please you.

So finally the house had mute grey verandahs added on, and a long trellis trailing with blue morning glories, looking like a veil floating from the house to the garage. An entirely modern wing was added onto the old house one year, with large windows overlooking the ravine so you could design your buildings in a place of solitude, yet still connected to your family. You would proudly take your clients on tours of the house that had started in two pieces, showing them the handmade hi-fi speakers built into the walls, the pale coral furniture your wife had recovered in the living room and office, your darkroom, the workshop in the garage with all the latest gadgets.

And yet the visitors must have wondered; there were never tricycles on the walks or toys in the hallways. If they had looked beyond the perfect flower beds through the basement windows they would have seen a laundry room with an old wringer washer standing on wooden blocks on the sloping floors and a confusion of protruding pipes and unfinished heating ducts. Any who followed the German's wife into the kitchen to thank her for the coffee and cake she always graciously produced would have noticed the kitchen cupboards, also handmade, but only partially painted, and how they seemed to be a sign of imbalance the family had adapted to over the years.

When the house that had defied completion for so long became too easy to finish, yes, that was it — when it became something the family could take for granted (wearing the same expression as the faces in church) — when your wife already had several fur coats and there were three sporty cars in the drive, then you took your visitors on a tour that included a vast area of the back yard. There, with a secret smile, as though you were uncovering a work of art, you would draw back the tarp on the emerging hull of a wooden sailing boat.

For months the heat from your bending the cedar ribs of the boat came blowing through our open windows. And for years afterward, the small wooden plugs (there were thousands and then thousands more) were found in stairwells, plugging bathroom sinks, nesting in toy boxes, and there was a light film of sawdust on the butter, on my mother's evening dresses, in the bowls of candies and nuts that sat uneasily in the darkened living room for guests that seldom came. As the hull of the boat grew, it seemed to take over the last recesses of our life which were not already spent in drawing lines or running a household forever at your beck and call.

The idea of a sailboat became an obsession. And you soon

neglected your career as an architect. You didn't even seem to care when there were fewer jobs and fewer clients. The fact that you were building an "ocean-going vessel," as you described it to others, seemed to be all that mattered. It seemed to reassure you, although not the angry contractors and developers, that the boat had both the beam and the freeboard to manage any ocean storm. Perhaps you were already far away on some watery horizon. You would often stand in the yard a long time when it was growing dark, the hull sleeping like a giant crustacean, like the last of an endangered species.

It's true you imagined your family of five leaving behind the dangers of modern life on shore and travelling long distances through all the charted waters on the maps you pinned up here and there in the house. You had modified the design of the Seafarer to make it just that much more practical and seaworthy for a family to live aboard, come hell or high water. But even on land, your dream was not without danger. Once there'd been molten lead for a two-ton keel waiting in huge vats, ready to be poured into the mold. Enough molten lead to drown a grown man, to cover and petrify the entire family of five. Toxic fumes rose on suddenly warm spring days, and poisonous paints for underwater surfaces stood here and there in open cans, tempting children and dogs. Droplets of varnish sprayed into unsuspecting eyes on windy days, sharp edges sliced off strips of skin, children's bikes rested against ladders about to fall. There were Skilsaws and drills on long extension cords waiting for victims.

Or at least that's how Mutti must have seen things as she looked with sadness at the gardens now neglected, almost three years of weeds growing around the boat cradle which had conquered the back yard. And we all suffered some of the perils — I sat on a huge, rusty spike one summer, which entered my leg on one side and poked through beneath my kneecap on the other, making my ankle sock fill with my own blood. And Martin, a young daredevil to match his father's large demands, fell steeply from the almost-finished sailboat to the steel crossbeams of the cradle and split his head wide open, laughing nervously when the blood ran warm through his white-blonde cap of hair. He acted weary and distant for days afterward, his sisters reading him Indian stories of war paint and tall corn and rain that never came from a book I still have somewhere. And my sister I remember as forever furious, her once-soft teenage hands calloused from the hours of varnishing and sanding, her fingernails short and choppy and blood-red with stain while other girls were painting theirs lilac and going to dances. And Mutti? She was watching over the people she loved. There was no rest for her — she had to see your dream complete and make certain we were all unharmed in the struggle.

Of course, you saw any sacrifice in the lives of your wife and children as small and insignificant compared with the beauty of the dream in which five wind-swept faces leaned together in the cockpit, the boat heeling dangerously somewhere near the island of New Caledonia in the Coral Sea, or at anchor in a quiet bay, the washing hanging from the boom, the smell of fish frying and the sound of muffled voices below carrying over the still water. And if the dream had in it some days of being becalmed on an ocean too wide to cross, or waves making the decks treacherous, perhaps even washing one of the five overboard — you never let on.

Yes, the dream was fierce. And obviously not for everyone. Strangers who stopped their cars on the street to see the family hammering and sanding and painting, or the neighbours who approached timidly from time to time, asking what you later called "stupid questions," seemed to linger until they sensed the danger, and then rushed off quickly with something urgent they had to do. Although they were tempted . . . I could see that. And you noticed it, too, how they were drawn in. They would lean on some freshly painted surface or step backward over a tool lying on the ground, and look pleased when the German included them, even for a moment, in the dream.

"Pass me the drill," you would say, or "The bag of two-inch nails. Over there. Over there." You sounded impatient and threatening, making them feel like one of the family.

And it worked both ways. Although you thought of the visitors as a nuisance, you could never resist nodding somewhat proudly when they mouthed their appreciation, "Super!" "Marvellous!" "Who drew up the plans?" "I did," you would say, grinning, your mouth full of nails. There was no doubt you were buoyed up by their admiration.

There they would stand, especially the men, talking of how fast she was, how much water she drew, how close to the wind she could tack, and loving to run their hands over the smooth, sweet-smelling hull, much like strangers like to touch a woman's pregnant belly. Sometimes the visitors would suddenly mention plans of their own, the house renovations they planned, or the antique cars that he loved and she'd have no part of. But something about the way the German would seldom answer, lowering his welding mask, the sparks making them jump aside, finally made them fidgety and cranky. And the visits would end with a sullen wish of good luck to a man who scarcely noticed them, their wives screaming at the children to get back into the car, fearful of losing a child to one of the dangers in such a place. And they would finally drive off, their faces looking back at the thirty-five-foot sailboat standing as tall as a house, pointing due west into the prevailing winds. And I always imagined them as somewhat relieved.

You would narrow your eyes at the departing strangers, and sneer. "Their children play hockey here, the others go to camp there, the wife plays bridge and the man plays golf, and what have they got?" you would ask. Handing one of your thin children a winch, forgetting how heavy a thing it was even for a grown man to hold. "They pay such high prices for a cottage in the summer, some little shack they have to drive hours to get to," you would say, "and we have it all here. Right here, Charlotte," you would say, your eyes squinting into the sun and some imaginary place on the horizon to which the word "here" extended. You would draw my mother closer then, and take her down below to show her some new feature in the galley. "You'll appreciate that when the nights are cold, you'll see," you would say to her, your hands running over the smooth mahogany. And you would emerge again up the short ladder, watching your son practising sailor's knots and taking the winch back from the girl who had held it for her father until her arms ached. And you would look to your wife again for approval of the scene, "Right here, Charlotte, we have something together."

My mother would always smile in agreement with you, or that was how it seemed anyway; her smile was always gentle and patient and rarely reproachful, even though she might have wished the visitors to stay longer sometimes, to lift her out of that place called "here." "Here" where she climbed ladders, her hair tied back with paint-spattered kerchiefs, "here" where she sat late at night covered with the yards of dacron sails she was endlessly sewing, then seat covers, then flags, "here" where there were always suppers to cook and clothes to wash and drawings to finish when the boat was finally left for the day.

For it was true, what the others said — you did not welcome outsiders. It was hard enough in those years of people letting go, husbands letting go of wives, mothers letting go of children, families letting go of their earlier dreams of making things fit. We never ate out (only stops to and from the yacht club at the Dairy Queen, because you had a soft spot for ice cream) because we could eat better at home, you said. But I think it was because it would keep us away from the others. Pure, our attention focused on you, still your family.

There were rarely children's voices playing on the paths around the house — they made too much noise, created too much uncertainty for the German to draw his lines. And since we were rarely allowed to visit others' homes — because of the work that needed to be done at home — we rarely played, except quietly in our rooms, or in places that drew little or no attention from you. My mother was left as policeman to make sure we didn't stray too far from the tasks you set us, and to see that we didn't get too close to your unfinished drawings. She was a gentle policeman. She would put her fingers softly to her lips, indicating with a sweep of her light blue eyes where you were, what mood you were in, what route to take to our own private pleasures. Often it was safest to sit with her in the kitchen while she cooked dinner and tell her quietly of school, of the friends we'd met, and look for support for some plan to go to a baseball game or have a friend in to play. "Let me talk to your father," she'd say.

But it was easier to wait for the days you went away early and returned late, visiting a building site somewhere. We left the house, scarcely stopping for a bite to eat, and lived as though each minute of the day counted two or three times, and talked incessantly and laughed too hard, and obeyed my poor mother very little. She scarcely seemed to mind, though, enjoying our freedom with us. We invited friends and had hot dogs and stayed out on our bikes, just talking, until dusk. Mutti would worry, of course, that you would return tired and in a foul mood from some struggle at the site and find your children in this state of random meals and vague curfew and full of high spirits. But the moment your car was seen pulling around the bend on Riverside Drive, we were all three in the back door and struggling to pull off sweaters and the smell of freedom before you should enter the house. The giggles, once again taboo, were scarcely stifled in time, the pyjamas were on with buttons done up the wrong way and hair uncombed. But you rarely noticed anything amiss. And we would fairly float to our rooms, overcome with the day's adventures. Savouring them.

For Mutti it must have been so much harder. She had few close friends; people seemed to be admitted to our enclave only to acknowledge our strength as a family. Only as witnesses. I know Mutti looked forward to these times — the times she could live for the moment. She would sit back and enjoy the *Krümelnkuchen* and strong coffee, the rare glasses of schnapps or German wines that were served on special occasions. She would turn with pleasure to all the voices mingling in the room, and glow in the randomness of the talk. And you, surprised by your wife's beauty then, and by her strength among the others, even you seemed to soften. Even you seemed to admit that the other voices had value, that your wife was your strong point, and you would smile at her then, quite openly, as though you loved her with all your might. Leaving behind your brittleness, you would hold the children close, forgiving us our trespasses of pouring spirits into our juices and getting drunk at dinner, of laughing too gaily in the midst of adult conversation, of staying up late just to have the feeling of connection to the outside world last and last and last.

But the people you admitted most readily, the two who came and went on alternate Sundays as regularly as aunt and uncle, were not blood relatives. The war had seen to that. You had no relatives except in passing remarks at the dinner table, remarks that revolved around the cruel hub of the word Hitler as regularly as the wheels of the trains that had carried everyone away. Your father, like Mutti's, had died on the Russian front, and your brother with the sticking-out ears had simply disappeared. Your own aunts and uncles, all gone. When your mother, the last of the family, had died of a kind of gnawing guilt in her gut that had finally been pronounced cancer and not simply war and worry, you had come to Canada. And there, in the first year, you had met Uncle and Lily. And with these two it was safe to tell the few stories that remained to be told.

The end of the war, the final day, that was really the only story that was ever told of the past. Probably because it alone seemed to lead out and away from Germany to the future. It was the one where the war was over and the young German, learning this, went to a clothesline near Raum and took off his uniform with a smile. . . . And one day, quite without warning, you told Uncle and Lily the story of the hoodlum boys too old for the eighth grade who had beaten up your eight-year-old daughter because she was born of a Nazi. You told them of your rage in the dead of winter when your own daughter had asked you what a Nazi was — the *a* pronounced with the sheep-like bleat of human shapes sent for slaughter, the *z* spoken smoothly and cruelly like the one in "razor."

I remember the day you told this story to Uncle and Lily, and the way you told it without any real sense of shame or guilt. I suddenly became ashamed that my schoolfriends had long called my father "the German." For as long as I could remember, the neighbours had done it, too, behind your back. But still loudly enough that your daughter could hear. And I was ashamed at how I'd come to think of you in this way, too, as though the world's mockery of your having been on the wrong side and having worn it so well made it still seem to stick. The world's mockery had extended cruelly even to your own daughter. Yes, I had sometimes called you the German too.

There is one scene I am most ashamed of, and it holds in it a few faces from my class, sitting on the steps after school, wasting time until the bus came. We had been speaking of fathers and I was typically quiet on the subject. But on that particular day, being egged on by their seeming unfairness to their own fathers, I took up the cause of the man we'd nicknamed "the German." I meant to tell them of the glory of fathers, of the glory we can scarcely see until the fathers are gone, but somehow I got it wrong. Or else it changed in the telling.

Anyway, I told the anecdote about my father driving the twenty or thirty miles between our house and the yacht club in Oakville, slowing down at every bridge along our route to measure whether the newly finished sailboat would ride safely on its passage from land to lake. "How did the German measure every bridge?" they asked. They were obviously curious about the man they'd never met, the man with the many talents and the serious outlook on life. I guess they remembered all the times they'd asked to walk me home or pick me up Saturday night for roller skating or to watch a ball game, and I'd said, "The German wouldn't like it." Rolling my eyes for the proper effect of suffering through my teens.

"Well —" I was savouring the effect this would have on my giddy friends. "Here I was in the back seat of the Corvair, holding a tall bamboo pole exactly fourteen feet, three inches high, the height of the boat on the trailer. And I had to hold the pole very straight or else the measurement would be off. And I could only imagine the German's anger if the boat should crack and splinter beneath some bridge on the day of its journey to the water. So I held the pole until my arms ached."

Of course by this time the kids were laughing themselves silly, imagining this girl as thin as the bamboo pole, imagining the passing cars looking on, but most of all imagining the stern face of the German, his eyes checking the straightness of the pole in the rear-view mirror. "You will hold the pole and you will enjoy it!" they all shouted in glee.

"Wait, I'm not finished," I said, my own face streaming with tears of laughter. "There were twenty-three bridges, I'm not kidding. But we get to this one bridge, narrower than the rest and therefore it seems tall, tall enough. Well, the German, he hardly slows down here, and the pole, it goes twang in my arms when we hit the bridge, and I almost get pulled out of the back window of the car with the vibration."

"Why didn't you let go of the pole?" the others shouted. They knew the answer, though: "The German wouldn't like it."

It was one of the few times I'd said such things about you, and had joined in with the others. I of course never mentioned how I loved you for your whacky ideas, for measuring bridges. After all, you were only protecting the boat you'd built those long years. But I never said how I admired you for your energy, sometimes even for your anger.

And I suppose I hadn't quite outgrown that awe and fear

of my own father as "the German," as the others saw you, when you disappeared from the face of the earth as surely as if your children had finally confessed about you to the authorities in your imagined scene of war. As though the daughter who'd once suffered on that winter road, the hoods pushing her down in the snow because she was connected to the man they named "the German," had finally turned you in.

I imagined the authorities, who were of course faceless and nameless — the hoods were just kids after all, who had learned their kind of condemnation from others before them — and who were somehow related to the word "Canada." Canada to a fifteen-year-old seemed big enough and abstract; it was a saddlebag-shaped place on a map in the geography room at school, full of Indians and mounted policemen and voyageurs and prime ministers — fourteen of them by the time you were declared dead and buried, like the others in Canada's history. Yes, Canada seemed so full of accidents and possibilities that it could have broken a man. I could see you had struggled with the loneliness of it, had finally seen the empty places to fill — with a wife, a brown house on four acres, with three cars, a boat, and enough money to send three children through school to make something of themselves, enough money not to worry as you had once worried in the war — as a kind of punishment. And I imagined the authorities watching carefully from behind the trunks of trees and from behind snow-covered cars, while you struggled this way, with something vague and huge and terrible, with Canada.

"Never doubt your parents, Else." The words rang in my ears, and I have since tried to imagine how the authorities had caught wind of my doubt, always kept so secret inside me.

Sometimes I think back to the summer I was four or five and sitting contentedly in the wading pool by the old brown shingle house. There is a day in that summer, a day that seems to me now a direct example of what happens to people when they are caught inside each other.

That morning I placed one wet jar inside the other and then

tried to pry them apart. The glass finally broke with all my twisting and pulling and the fragments cut my wrists so that the water in the little pool turned all crimson. Mutti, looking out the kitchen door with that smile that protected me from things like this, shrieked then and ran to me in a way that made her clothes fly back. And she splashed that red water all around trying to move the glass away from her child. Then, pressing my wrists here and there, she carried me to the house, the blood running down the apron she always wore. The blood running into the gardens we passed, I quite white and shaken, and somehow curious to see what would happen next. Although I never cried.

Mutti blamed herself, it was clear, and she wept that day several times. Not for what had happened but for what she imagined could have been lost in one brightly lit moment of mid-morning. To a little girl that event seemed a strange and early example of how easily love can be strained in a mother's face. Reflecting to me for the first time how love was a hard thing and a heavy thing.

Years later I could say that the event had ended happily in the sense that the cuts were all superficial and that I, as that small child, had been less frightened than puzzled. But a strange thing happened as a result of that day, and I began then to see that thing happening more and more.

Everyone who heard of the morning in the wading pool had a different way of talking about it. Mutti spoke of it as though she herself had put the glass jars within the reach of her small daughter to harm her. And she blamed herself anew in every telling of it. You, Vati, told it as though the glass jars were immaterial and agreed that Mutti was somehow the culprit. And perhaps to some extent you also blamed the curiosity of the child, trying to make things fit. You grew impatient whenever Mutti mentioned it again, which she did for some time, because she would find a small spot of blood on the doorframe or on the sunflowers by the back stairs that would remind her.

One of your neighbours laughed as Mutti brought it up again one day. Mutti said later that perhaps the woman's laughter had something to do with her four-year-old boy dying of whooping cough earlier that same year, as if that explained it.

In any case it was simply a series of actions whenever I recalled it. And I remembered it clearly. I was simply playing in the shallow pool, half in shade and half in sun, on a warm summer's day, and I stepped out of the pool to see a caterpillar that was clinging to a twig on the ground. I watched the caterpillar for some time, tickling it with the twig. And then, catching sight of Mutti checking out the door for my whereabouts, I felt some guilt at the curled-up caterpillar shape and I went where she couldn't see me, shouting, "I'm here, Mutti," to reassure her as I went.

For some reason I knew even then that something was going to happen. I could feel it like I could feel the water droplets in the small of my back and I shivered as I went through the basement door into the concrete room I was a little afraid of for no particular reason. The floor was cold and I went to your workbench and simply stood looking at the tools there. Some, like the hammer hanging on the wall, caught the small amount of light coming through the window. Some I could only feel in the dark, like the saw, which turned around through the wood with a sharp sound that made my teeth grit. It was there somewhere in the dark and I had been warned about that.

So I stood for a few minutes, thinking of your hands holding those tools because they belonged to you and it seemed that the smell of sawdust and of those things in tins that smelled strong and bad were a private thing of yours. And they would be mine some other day. Not today. And above me, in the house, I heard Mutti talking on the phone to someone and I smiled to hear her voice.

And then right there in front of me, on a shelf tucked in below the wooden bench, were all these jars, some sticky with stiff paintbrushes in them, some with the labels of my favourite jam, some so dusty I didn't want to touch them, and even one with a spider in it. And right behind the spidery one, so that I had to reach around behind it carefully, were two jars that looked somehow clean. That small light from the window had fallen on them and made them shine a little. And they seemed just the right size and cleanness and shape to be taken with me and used for some game in the pool.

So I took them carefully, one in each hand, and carried them back into the sunlight, feeling relieved that I had found them as I sank happily back into the warm water again. It was only a moment later that Mutti came to the door and smiled at me, never seeing the glass jars. Only a moment after that, when the jars were stuck, one inside the other, Mutti looked again, seeing the reddened water and the look of surprise on her daughter's face. I was simply sitting quietly watching the blood drift in a warm red circle around me.

So to me the stories they all began to tell of that morning were somehow false. And unnecessary. No one was to blame or had done anything wrong, as far as I could see.

Only now, as I'm past thirty, and I think back to my childhood, there are stories that rear their heads and want to come between myself and what must have happened. And I'm frightened that somewhere along the line I have slipped into the thing they all did the day I played with the glass jars. That I now find the stories necessary. I find I have to struggle to keep the glass jars mere objects in a child's pool.

Few other things besides the glass jars have remained clear. One thing I haven't tampered with, although I feel older in this memory and impressions already carry a certain weight, is the good-night game. The game where I stepped carefully on the narrow yellow patches of light that slid underneath the doors and fell along the hallway. The game where I could have run back at any time to my room if I'd wanted to; that had remained an unspoken rule of survival. But in all the years of stepping on the bands of light, I had never retreated.

When I reached the dark part of the hallway where the stairs came down overhead, turned, and fell away again below, Martin was often there waiting for me. And usually after we whispered together for a while we both went into the room that opened out of that corner. It felt somehow easier for us to go into that room together.

This is the way I remember my brother in the game: sitting on the top stair that led to the cellar, his knees pulled up to his chest, his face seeming white and far away like the parts of his body that didn't fit into his pajamas because he had grown again. Part of the game was asking him whether he'd been in yet to say good night and he sometimes whispered yes and he sometimes whispered no until that part of the game fell away because the answer didn't really matter anymore.

I remember once when he said no, that he wouldn't go. Not that night, not ever again. I felt his despair but at the same time I felt my own excitement that I would go in alone. We sat together for a time leaning toward the door to listen for the sounds from inside the room. First we heard the pencil sharpener, then a book being closed. When we didn't hear anything more I smiled at him and he passed me a red candy which he'd been holding in his hand. I took that as a sign that things would be different that night, for usually he brought me a green or a purple one because those had been my favourite colours for as long as I'd been a child.

When I sucked on the sticky candy it made a loud popping noise in my cheeks and we both started to laugh, gripping each other desperately so that the laughter would stop. So we wouldn't be discovered like that in the part of the game that had always given us courage.

Right after that he looked sad again and said he wished we could hide somewhere together. I remember that plainly because I thought it generous of him to want to protect me, even in that obscure way.

And yet he must have known I would only knock gently on the door as always. That I would open the door just far enough to avoid hitting the small table that held the typewriter and then drag my toes so they left soft-looking marks in the old carpet. There was a green tree in the pattern of the rug, which I'd always stood on at the place under the dark purple flowers on the branches. He had watched me often enough.

On that night I did all those things Martin could imagine me doing and when you didn't turn around I pretended to look at all the books that surrounded you like stones in a high, impenetrable wall. But really I was looking at you. The lamp that hung above your head shone on your hands, too, and made them seem separate from your face, drawn tight in the circle of light, and from your body, arched in the semi-dark. The hands were what I was after.

Some nights when the hands were not drawing long, straight lines on the white sheets of paper that were held with thumbtacks onto the slanting table, those hands drew horses for me. Horses with large flaring nostrils, one leg prancing in front, a tail zigzagging behind. Your horses ended up looking a little like your houses and your churches and your schools, although they began with circles inside the cheekbones, the shoulders, the haunches, instead of straight lines. Their shapes were half circle, half straight line, I had decided. Which made your horses look finally more like terrible machines than the soft plodding animals in my storybooks. But the dangerous look of them, and the way you sometimes held my smaller hand in yours to draw them like that, was what I wanted.

But the nights of horses had been rare. I had had to wait hard for them.

That night you cleared your throat with the scratchy noise and turned your chair with the silent little silver wheels so that you could look down at me. I knew right away it would not be a night for horses simply because you didn't seem to see me at all. You seemed to be looking at something far away that often kept you quiet until I pressed shut the door of your room again. You kissed me then, as you always did, and left the same feeling of cold on my forehead that always made me want to cringe, although I never had.

But on that night I couldn't help shivering and my wish for the day you would pick me up again and put me on your lap seemed to run up and down my body. And because I suddenly felt like crying and you always got angry when I cried, I turned and ran toward the door. In my hurry to leave the room I knocked your black leather case, holding a compass and plastic triangles, from a table, and I bent down to the carpet, searching frantically for all the pieces. I listened for the creaking of the chair back, which would have meant you were leaning forward over your table again and had perhaps not even noticed. But the room was so quiet that I looked up, my face ashamed. You were smiling at me, and I thought your face looked happy, especially your eyes. And that look had been more rare than the nights of horses.

Outside in the dark hallway I knew Martin had gone. I wanted him still there, to confide in him, encourage him. I was sure Mutti, feeling his sadness there on the stair, had taken him to bed, or else he would have waited for me.

Mutti had turned off all the lights on her way upstairs, and so there were no more places to put my feet on the way back to my room. That had always been the last part of the game.

PART V

Lovers

The last snowstorm in Alberta can happen as late as May. She feels sorry that she has to meet him again this way, the first time, in a snowstorm before the first flowers. When she sees Dean come over the crest of the rise on 99th Street, she has this odd sensation that he is coming home. Even though she no longer knows where home is. But he's had to abandon his car several blocks away where it's stalled, that's all. So she offers him a ride.

Before long they are sitting in a restaurant, a new avant-garde place in Edmonton called The Prava. Not that the furniture is new; the wooden tables are old and cracked, the chairs are mismatched café style with bentwood backs and frayed wicker seats that have taken the shape of the most loyal customers. It's the kind of place where people often read books for hours, ordering *café latté* until the machine breaks down. Which it often does. But it has stacks of foreign newspapers and it's also a good place for old lovers to size each other up, be a little reckless with their pasts.

Of course when he asks her what she's been up to, she knows he doesn't want to hear about her father. That was just the thing that had made him angry. So she reassures him, tells him it's over, her "love affair with doom and gloom," as he once called her obsession with the past.

"I'm cured of my lisp," she says, careful not to slam her tongue against the back of her teeth.

"Your lisp?" he asks carefully, afraid for a moment that she is leading him into one of her traps.

And she explains how she always had a real snarl in the *s* sound whenever she mentioned her father out loud. She probably did it out of nervousness as a child when she was talking to him, she says to Dean. "So for years it's been as though everything were still a dialogue with my father."

Dean doesn't say a thing. She used to wonder whether he saw the connections to his past in the way he stroked his beard for comfort or gradually grew despondent whenever she beat him at Scrabble. It was years before she found out that he'd had a bad bout with mononucleosis as a child, and had continually played board games with his mother, giving up listlessly somewhere before the end.

She knows it's a habit of old lovers to go back over the events of their last day together, but she thinks it's an unhealthy one. No one can convince her that it isn't just a way of setting the record straight; he raised his hand, therefore she. . . .

But that is simply not true. It is some gesture long before the scene in which they are separated by a body of water, which seemed a lake and was only a bath. The hand that came between them was her own, the one she had allegedly raised in order to kill a man. She wants to finally come clean on that one; she wants to finally let Dean know that she has never really tried to kill anyone. That she is innocent.

At least it will be better than accusing Dean of being a lukewarm lover, which is the other thing that occurs to her, how she blames him for having always remembered to pull out chairs for her, open doors, and her birthdays (at least after the very smallest reminders), having placed the hope in her that a lukewarm lover could last a lifetime. He always intended it to be enough that he was simply faithful.

But his love was never rash, headlong, the kind of love

around which all other decisions took their places. No, his lukewarm love always set its own standards. For a long time she has known there would never be any consequences. There would never be childbirth or any other bloodbaths between them. In fact, lukewarm love would fade away if you let it — things fall apart easily enough — and growing to be good friends, that was probably the best a pair of lukewarm lovers could ever be together. But that would take years of forgetting what there was beyond the act of lukewarm love.

But rather than say any of that — she would have been made to look foolish in admitting she once wanted to give Dean presents of braided flowers, falling to her knees to clasp a man around the legs — she orders steak tartar, Dean wrinkling his nose up at the smell of raw meat, and they drink several carafes of surprisingly good wine.

She mentions the dream with the ferris wheel then. "You were in it," she says, although she doesn't mention the transformation; the father figure, wise, gentle, the man she has always wanted to meet, seeming for a startling moment to be Dean. Carl Jung as an architect, laying the cornerstone for marriage.

For a moment she can see the dream unfolding; she sees herself running a nervous hand along the edge of the old table at The Prava, a hand that requires only a golden wedding band, and looking hard at the gold specks in Dean's otherwise jade-coloured eyes. After five years of trying to combine apparently disparate male and female elements, she can see them performing some kind of alchemical ritual, sifting through the remaining ashes, looking for the effects of combining not sulphur and quicksilver, but drawing tubes and dreams, snow shovels and bathtubs, his future and her past, his myriad facts and her pressing fantasies. . . . She can imagine Jung poring over old texts, which described the "chemical marriage" of a king and a queen who are killed through their union, only to rise again, transformed. Hence the ancient belief that a marriage in a dream means a death, she wants to say to Dean, and that a death in a dream means a marriage.

Of course she knows Dean doesn't believe in dreams as portents. She imagines he sees them as a kind of underwater sport or a safari into wild African territory. You simply pay for a scuba teacher or a good guide with silent footfalls and sharp eyes to get you out of scrapes. But it is not territory for an amateur explorer, and thus better left alone.

But she doesn't have to worry; Dean leaps at the chance to avoid confrontation. He starts telling her about the first ferris wheel, at the Columbian World Exposition in Chicago in 1893. He tells her the damn thing was so big — 250 feet in diameter, 825 feet in circumference, 30 feet wide — that each of its cars held 40 passengers, the giant wheel capable of holding 1,440 people in total. He draws a replica of one of the cars on his paper napkin — it looks somewhat like an old train car, made of wood and iron, with glass windows, and swivel seats for the joy riders, Dean says. When he can see she's becoming impatient he insists quite eagerly that the riders paid only fifty cents to enjoy two full revolutions of the wheel, and that it was a great success. Designed by an unassuming civil engineer named George Washington Gale Ferris, it ended up being Chicago's answer to the Eiffel Tower.

He obviously hasn't seen the risk involved. For Else breaks in, reminding him of the women's pavilion at that same fair. She explains that it stood near the midway, that one left the noise and bustle of the mile-long strip of amusements, passed over a bridge, to arrive at a serene building crowned with sculpted female forms pulling away from the roof, wings sweeping back from the soft robes that clung to their stone bodies and from their long, flowing hair, a building filled with light and silence and surprising exhibits.

"What kind of exhibits?" he asks, feeling how they have suddenly come full circle, back to that first uneasy day they spent together at the women's festival in Saskatoon.

"Soft things and hard things," she says, giving him a

generous smile that seems to eclipse five years of feeling it was hopeless between them. "Laces and bed quilts, the large basket-like palanquin a woman explorer had slept in on the slopes of Kilimanjaro, charcoal-fired knives collected from the Masai, the model of a leper village in Siberia, marble busts of poker-faced feminists, and an iceless milk cooler, the Flynt Waist Corset, the safety elevator."

"No rope spinners?" he asks, a smile wedged between his beard and the look of relief in his eyes. He must have expected to hear the anger in her voice, the old anger.

She takes a deep breath; suddenly it seems they are right back at the beginning. It's like having a second chance at the same story, except this time it will be summer, and this time the gun she holds will be an act of mercy. Of forgiveness. It is a story still intact, still capable of carrying the truth forward. After all, Dean has never heard of the summer before he met her, the summer of the Dutch boys.

Dean knows little else besides the fact that she worked as a waitress in a pub on the outskirts of a small Ontario town in a summer so hot the men drank harder than usual. She must have told him she wanted to buy the farm without indoor plumbing, one of the oldest in the area. She once showed him a book written about that same farm in Hastings County, the one farmed by a series of strong-minded settlers, the Tivys, the Godbolts, the McGregors. The book was actually a collection of letters written by a lonely pioneer woman who'd been saddled with five children and the cares of the farm when her husband had died from the kick of a horse. Dean showed little interest in the story at the time.

She remembers reading several of the letters out loud to him, being angry with him for the fact that he couldn't sense that woman's loneliness, feel her being drawn toward defeat. She eventually moved back to England after burying several of the children on the farm, and Else remembers riding around the old logging trail that surrounded the three hundred acres of farmland, looking for any sign of the graves.

She never found any headstones or crosses, but there were times in that summer that she discovered what that pioneer woman had left behind.

She wants to tell Dean how it feels when a woman's alone. She knows she won't say all she remembers aloud, and that Dean won't always hear what she says. But she wants Dean to begin to understand.

So she tells him of that last night on the farm, how she could feel the summer ending. She was washing by the pump, as usual, stripped to the waist. The air seemed cool, as though autumn were just days away. She was rubbing herself briskly with the towel, to stay warm.

She could hear their tractor idling furiously and she could feel the eyes and thoughts of the three brothers on her back. They were always watching her, the Dutch boys across the road. The squeal of the anxious wooden pump handle would warn them to stop what they were doing and watch her strip to the waist and wash. She always did this just before seven o'clock. By eight she had left a cloud of dust down the road that left their throats dry with desire.

She imagined they resented her. But could not put her out of their minds. After all, she existed; they'd seen her in the daylight hours with the cows and the horses, mending fence. Lifting the huge stones back into position, using split cedar rails to fill in the gaps where the work was too heavy. Or pushing the wheelbarrow along the ridge and tipping it slowly, carefully, at the top of the embankment, where she let the manure slide into the well-managed piles of old, and fresher, fertilizer. And in the evenings she'd given them large, cool pitchers of beer and they had all looked away mutely, shame for what they were thinking flushing red up the backs of their necks where the sun had shone too much, as on their bright blonde heads of hair.

And of course they had seen her washing every night before going into town. Out there by the pump in the dusk. And still she washed there, knowing the boys were watching, with her naked like that, sometimes to the waist, sometimes to the place her bare feet stood in the wet pool on the ground. Let them watch, she had thought so many times, pouring the cold water in a curtain down her breasts and over her arms. They were so far away, what could they see anyway? She had turned her back on them that way so often, and yet she could feel the danger in their watching.

She thought of them as boys, but they were really men, still living at home, the eldest son her age, in his mid-twenties. Their lives hard, she knew, because they were contained within the limits of all that backbreaking labour their father dished out. She'd heard the old man yelling some nights; his hoarse Dutch syllables reached right across the quarter-section when one of the boys did something wrong. And she could feel their shame then as they ate their suppers indifferently and later stretched out flat on their beds, stiff with desire for a way beyond their pastures, the insides of their heads washing with beer.

Some nights the sound of a horn had come from their farm, a sound floating unattached to the rest of the day, to the people living there. She tried to guess for a long time which son it was that blew so hard into the trumpet, trying to change the rock-littered fields and the quiet farmhouse into something else. The sound that came less and less often as the summer passed. Too much to do, she thought bitterly, on that last day. Or not enough to play for.

She'd gone there several times, where the Dutch boys lived, up their long, neatly trimmed driveway. The mother — she was called Astrid — kept one of those houses neat as a pin, with the smell of eternity baking in the oven and the flower beds always blooming right on time. Once she'd asked the Dutch woman for advice in making preserves from the quince that grew, strangely exotic, by her back door. Astrid was cutting wafer-thin licorice into small black triangles. "It's poisonous if you eat it off the trees," she said. "But it makes good jelly."

Another time she'd wanted to borrow a drill bit from the old man. At first he said no, that he didn't want his bits broken. And then as she was walking away he ran after her in his wide-topped rubbers and offered her the whole metal case with twenty or more bits in it. "I suppose you know what to do with them," he said brusquely.

Each time she'd walked up that long driveway she felt what the whole family believed in, needed to believe, to still be living like that. She felt it in the formal way they greeted her, in their stiff offers to help. In some way they believed they were helping her morally when they reached out a spade to her, or a pickling jar. And in some way she even longed for the formidable family weight that hung dumbly in the eyes of those three brothers. Each time she came to call they walked her grimly back down the drive, as though seeing her safely off their property and away from their own temptation. Back into the distant scene in which they watched her washing.

She'd often tried to talk to them on those long walks down the lane, but they only nodded or shrugged or smiled uncertainly, looking up at the sky for reassurance. Noting the future in one-word warnings of bad weather. And when they reached the road and she looked toward her own farmhouse (measuring how small the pump seemed from where they stood), she often wondered whether to say thank you, call them by name, touch them briefly on a hand or an arm. Or simply say goodbye. But they always turned so quickly whenever they sensed her hesitation there beneath the rattling poplars, and she watched them walk with big, awkward strides away from her questions.

Did they ever imagine what she knew of them? That she could feel their pride in that family and their shame? That she despised their retreat to the sacred hearth that kept them weary, their young backs already slouching with the years of bending over crops and machinery when they should have simply been growing tall. She remembers how surprised she'd been the first time she saw them up close, how tall they were standing next to the huge eight-hundred-pound round bales. She watched them roll those colossal bales as though they were light sleeping bags of freshly mown grass.

"Yeah, the hay'll be fine like that," she said lamely when the three boys drove up with the first cut from her lower fields, leaving her enough for the half a dozen cows and the two horses. But she cursed them for a time whenever she pulled the hay apart in soft, unwieldy waves, wrestling it into the mangers. Then it began to seem right that way, as though the hay had simply walked off the fields and come to lie before the animals at feeding time. Moving a little in the wind that blew through her drafty old barn, as though it were still growing.

She remembered the evening the horses had gotten into the hay field, galloping up and down in the scent of it like two mad things while the Dutch brothers across the way watched in disapproval. She let the horses run until they tired, snorting and whistling in their feeling of the approaching dark and summer drawing to a close, finally standing quiet, the long grass reaching to their heaving flanks. And she knew the Dutch boys thought to themselves, along with their father, "Just like a woman to go ruining hay like that. Just like a woman." And still she sat with the last sun slanting down on her, her legs astride the split rail fence, laughing at the horses. Just sitting there and laughing.

Oh, it wasn't that they weren't desirable, those three boys turning into men so gravely. They were lean and muscled and they were easy enough with the world when they were working in the fields. That's when she was watching. But still she knew it was as hopeless from where she watched as it was the other way around. She knew you didn't change men who hadn't changed from the stiff-necked ways of the past. And that to make love to them would be asking for that change. And asking for a whole lot of misunderstanding and perhaps even anger.

She knew all the boys were going to leave one day; one of

them angry, one of them simply tired, and one (perhaps the youngest) somewhat lost, and leave farming behind. Never marrying the girls from similar upbringings and similar mealtime tables they were intended to meet. Finally moving toward the thing inside them that was telling them to show interest in a young woman on the next farm. Finally leaving behind the rigid shape of family that convened by force and by deadened ritual.

It was strange, on that last night she welcomed their watching. She felt a shiver when they turned back toward their mother's house, the windows full of light. For it was then she heard the sound. The brushing sound of overalls, jeans, coming through the long grass. The sound of boots slurring on the gravel of the drive. She gasped. Drew the towel tightly around her.

Of course she'd had a warning of something about to end. The meat man had come for the old thoroughbred with the bad tendon that morning. She got almost nothing for him because she wanted him shot first; no way that old horse was going to stand in line with the other horses at the meat packers' and take his turn, smelling all that death around him. The meat man, unshaven, and unwilling to take the horse any other way but alive, finally agreed, and shot the horse twice in the head while he was grazing.

She smiled sadly to remember how she gave the old horse the best grass on his last morning, letting him wander through the front garden and the hydrangeas fading from the summer's heat, his old teeth pulling only the most tender shoots here and there. He must have thought he was already there, in paradise. Even before his still bay body was slowly winched into the blood-smeared truck, his great old race-horse head with the white blaze bumping up the ramp and out of sight.

So she should have known when the men came like that, their clothes smelling of freshly spread manure and their mouths smelling of drink, that there would be trouble. It was almost dark; they were on their way home from the bar. Several of the men she knew vaguely, and she knew, too, that they weren't married or anything. In fact it surprised her how many men were working the land, even alone. Even without the nagging debt of wives and children to worry about along with the thin soil and the tyranny of the weather. And that night, the last night on the farm, the farmers lonely for wives came calling.

She recognized one of the men as the young, stoop-shouldered fellow who'd driven his pick-up into the elm at the fork of the main road not long ago. He still had a scar; the new skin shone like a halo around his forehead. And she said hello to another, a middle-aged widower she'd given a blue heeler pup to a few months back. When she smiled at him, he took it as a sign — he put his hand on her side just below her breast. "We're here to see if you need anything, like I said to the boys." The others laughed. "We want to be good neighbours, is all," he added when he sensed her fear through his hand rising and falling on her fast breathing. She counted them then; six of them, and no sympathy anywhere in any of their faces.

She shook off the widower's hand with a laugh and a sideways glance designed to give the drunk men some hope. "I haven't seen you boys at the bar lately," she said, taking her dirty flannel shirt from the pump handle and pulling it over her head as the men watched. Their eyes flickered a little in the heavy light just past sunset as they saw the towel fall, her shoulders and the tips of her breasts disappearing into the man's shirt.

"You haven't been lookin'," said a sour-faced young farmer, the others laughing their nervous laughter again.

"Can we come in? We're tired," whined another, older-looking face, although his hair was black and greased back without any signs of grey.

"I was just going out, actually. To check some stock over at the neighbour's." She walked with the men slowly down the drive toward the main road, her bare feet leaving soft, fragile-looking prints in the dust.

"We'll keep you company," a mean voice said.

"Guess I'm lucky," she whispered, keeping her eyes on the farm of the Dutch family a half mile or so across the fields like a point of rescue in her mind. Measuring the steps she'd already taken from the house, how many more before she would reach the main road, looking down the fence line across the south field where the boys so often were this time of night. Measuring what would happen if the men grabbed her right then and took her into the bushes looming dark on the side of the road. Imagining how her voice would sound stretched out across those fields; like an animal's, hit hard by fear and pain. And she measured what she knew of the three brothers, and what they knew of her, whether they would recognize her voice, turn toward it.

She imagined what they knew of her, besides the washing. They probably knew she'd slept with the men from the pub band that was in town only a few days; not just with the short, dark-eyed drummer who was studying law and smelled of another woman when he pulled her mouth down on him, but also with the tall one, who rode her much the same way he'd ridden the horses. He left her skin caked with sweat and her breathing ragged one afternoon right after the thunderstorm, and then he went away. That night she washed longer than usual beside the pump, trying to rinse the salt and weariness from her before the mosquitoes came out at dusk.

They might have also known about the policeman who came to deliver a parking ticket one morning, staying for coffee, the way it happens in small towns. Who left the farmhouse hours later and shouted goodbye too loudly. So that his triumphant voice rang across the fields much like the bull's that the Dutch boys kept across the road. She imagined they knew what happened when she came to the door that morning wearing only a flannel nightgown, her long dark hair smelling of wood smoke, the everpresent smoke that made the lace curtains in the house seem to hold sooty shadows, even in bright sunlight.

Then the cop came by a second time, uninvited. Walked

right into her kitchen on a bright summer morning. She came running from the garden when she heard the snarling and the shout, but by then her bitch just new with pups had taken a piece out of him. There he stood, looking so large and helpless, an L-shaped tear in his pants, a nasty blue bruise already swelling on his pale skin. She leaned in the doorway and laughed. The dog had bitten him right in the hip that had descended on her so hard again and again.

She didn't see him after that. And she imagined he boasted then about his unlikely conquest in her house, as men will who have lost their pride.

Probably the Dutch boys also knew of the doctor who lived several concessions west. He started out by letting her use his shower. The Dutch boys had only to imagine the first and last days of that affair; it wasn't long before she was washing once more by the pump.

There were two more she could scarcely remember by the summer's end, although the Dutch boys might remember their sudden arrivals in an early spring. One was a cabdriver who had played a guitar and had read Damon Runyon stories to her on the front steps. For a time she believed she might be in love with him; they argued about practically everything. And then there was the restless man she'd gone camping with, who admitted to her somewhere in those endless hours of rolling around in a sleeping bag that he was a professional bicycle thief.

She is counting lovers in the warm, compressed darkness of the restaurant, Dean meanwhile looking out to the blizzard, tipping back in his chair, as though he is balanced somewhere between what he already knows of her and what she wants him to discover. She's afraid to continue with the story, afraid that Dean will look at her from a distance, as the Dutch boys had always done. For her greatest fear that night was that the Dutch boys might find her too indecent to save.

She walked with the half a dozen men, the same number as her lovers in that summer, feeling desperately alone in those miles of farmland uncertain with bogs and outcroppings of rock. They reached the end of the drive and still no sign of the Dutch boys, as she'd hoped. Only darkness closing in. Cows mooing for comfort in the dusk.

"She sure likes walking. Wonder what else she likes." The men laughed again, the kind of laugh they used when a cow was down and there was nothing more to be done. One of them grabbed her shoulder, and she turned quickly, her arm burning from the pressure of his hand. It was then she saw the gun, lying in the tall grass by the side of the road like a dark branch. The meat man's rifle.

All she could hear was the men breathing heavily around her, and the piercing seesaw of the crickets. She remembers thinking that the anger and the fear would soon be flowing both ways, and then the feeling right after, that it was impossible. That she would never reach the gun, that it would misfire, that the men would scatter and ambush her, using the gun then in their rough game of manhood.

She was about to run when she saw the truck come fast down the summer-hard surface of the dirt road. "Hey, John!" she shouted, stepping in front of the speeding truck and waving both arms. The truck braked, sending up loose gravel from the shoulder as it swerved, and stalled. A face she recognized peered suspiciously from behind the wheel. It was John, the oldest brother, and she knew by the way he looked away that he wouldn't save her. That he and the figure too dark to make out in the cab were about to pull the truck around the men huddled like a strayed herd on the road, and pass her. Leave her there.

"Hey, John," one of the men behind her mimicked, holding her around the waist. She pushed him away and reached for the door handle of the truck, already grinding into gear and pulling away. She swung up into the moving cab, saying thanks breathlessly, as though there'd been an unspoken agreement about a lift into town, and looked at the faces of the two brothers beside her. They only stared straight ahead, past the men blinking foolishly in the headlights. The truck sped up with a whine, and she pressed her cheek against the cold glass and stared out at the dark. Someone butted out a cigarette, western music wailed from the radio, and no one said a thing the five or six miles to town. But she could feel the thigh of the youngest brother pressed close and warm against her in the cramped cab.

When they parked at the Legion she simply thanked them. The way she'd often meant to after they'd walked her home. She thought then she might say something else — about the way their father shouted at them, or about their living at home — just kidding them somehow, trying to show her sympathy for them. She'd often imagined walking down the driveway with them, the sun slanting through the poplars, their faces breaking into grins, their eyes showing relief to finally find her a colleague in the hardship that was home — but each time she'd imagined this (and sometimes she'd seen them all laughing, their long arms flung around her shoulders, her waist, all laughing), each time she'd finally remembered their defended postures, the way they pulled up their shoulders a little when she spoke to them and the way they felt it was all only about sex. So she knew that night would be no different. That it was useless to even begin. The eldest brother nodded, the truck doors slammed with a hollow sound, and no one said a thing more.

The story does not end with the Dutch boys knowing how a woman feels who's alone. They probably felt somehow that she deserved the bad attention that came her way. The story does not even end with the angry mob of men hoisting her back gate high up on a power pole. When she came home from town at midnight she had to collect the cows from the marsh down the old logging road. She noticed then that one was missing.

Somehow she knew the story had to end with the gun, still lying in the grass. Certainly the meat man would come back for it, probably early the next day. Surly and short-tempered that he'd left it behind like that. And then everything would be back to where it had been before. Except she knew she would probably get another. That she needed a gun if she was to stay.

She decided she had to leave the farm, by morning, or sooner. In the middle of that night, which had become the last night, she began to gather together all her belongings by the front door; it looked somewhat like a child intending to run away from home. Among the pots and pans, blankets, lamps, there was also a sorry rocking horse with empty eye sockets and the real horsehair mane she'd snipped off when she was four, a sweater with red trim and wooden buttons her mother had once made for her — was she saving it for a daughter, or a son? — a duffel bag almost emptied now of the few things her mother had saved, and the butterfly chair, its bright yellow wings folded up. It was as she was taking down the lace curtains, thinking of her stealing them as a kind of tribute to the pioneer woman, that she saw the shadow pass by the house. A shadow in the shape of a man.

It was odd how she recognized him, the youngest of the three, the one who always seemed the laziest in his eyes, as though his life might not be touching him, twisting him, as much as it seemed to wring the others' looks. He was standing close by the window. Watching her. She couldn't think why he'd come, couldn't think of a rake she'd had too long, or a cake tin she hadn't returned to his mother's steamy kitchen, warm as a womb.

His mouth seemed to frame a question he didn't ask. She might have been imagining it, but she had the feeling he'd been standing there some time, watching her pack. Feeling her sadness, her anger.

They both moved toward the door then, he walking through the quiet dark, she moving through the house with all the rooms bright, holding the lace curtains like the fragile evidence of a series of women who had left the farm. Perhaps also feeling afraid, deciding too quickly what to take or leave behind, never feeling the pain of the last night until much later.

"I thought I should tell you," he said lamely when she met him at the door, holding it open for him.

"Tell me?"

She felt like saying it didn't matter anymore, that this was the last night. That she was leaving. Perhaps he'd come to tell her he'd admired her for some time now. Perhaps the youngest was going to make a move on his brothers and tell her something she'd waited all summer long to hear. The youngest always prospered in the fairy tales.

"My father made a deal with Clarence."

Clarence was the small, bitter-hearted man who owned the farm, a man who'd lost the fingers on both his hands one winter when he'd fallen asleep dead drunk only ten feet from his own back door. He lived on a disability pension now, in town, and came to the farm every now and then just to tell her stories about how the place had looked in its prime. He threw the animals feed sometimes, using only his palms with the blunted finger stumps to try to lift the hay.

"So your father wants the farm? Well, I don't care anymore. You can have the cows." Her voice was as dead and flat as the miles of poor farmland parched by the heat.

Apparently the boy wasn't finished. He looked down to the road, and seemed to listen. "There's a cow, one of yours — she's down, and she's having some trouble calving. Thought I'd tell you," he said, standing awkwardly close.

"Does your father know?"

"He says he won't help. That's it's your job. That you should have done something before now — she's so overdue. So I came to help."

"Damn your father and damn the cow. Why couldn't she have waited one more day until I was gone?" She sneered at him then. "Where are your brothers? Don't they want to see me deliver a calf?"

"Well, Binke and John laughed when I said I was going to

help. They said you'd rather do it on your own. But the cow looks bad, and I thought you might still be in town — so I came."

She turned away. The youngest was talking against his brothers; the youngest was trying to be fair with an indecent woman. And somewhere a cow was burning with her unborn calf out in the darkness of the field.

It was true, it was her fault. The cow was long past calving time; now the calf had missed the summer sun and had only the thin grass and cool days of autumn to grow in. But something had kept her from going up the long tree-lined drive and asking the Dutch boys for help.

She let the front door slam behind her. She was already six or seven strides ahead of the boy, her anger keeping the distance between them intact. She walked lightly through the mud that never seemed to dry up in the barnyard, stopping at the shed to pick up a lantern and what looked like a carpenter's apron, with a knife, clean gauze, and some disinfectant wrapped in plastic in the pockets. The sound of the boy's heavy work boots followed her.

She struck a match for the lantern and winced as it flared against her hand. She looked up to see whether he'd noticed. Their eyes met as she handed him the light. "Where is she?"

He led her to the cow that lay by the watering hole, her flanks moving raggedly in and out, her hind legs kicking erratically in contractions too close together, too hard.

"I'm sorry. I know you wanted the place. I'm sorry," he repeated, "and I told my father it was wrong after the work you did here."

She was surprised by the boy's words and by his long arm reaching into the cow's womb. The cow bellowed and the boy's brow was furrowed. "You're going to lose the calf soon," he said. "And the cow is probably done for anyway. Give me the knife."

He tapped the swollen belly on the cow with his fingers, listening to the sound, as though she were an ancient instrument. Then he slashed the hide above the womb as expertly as a butcher in a meat shop. The cow moaned once or twice and lay still, steam rising from the warm incision, her head flat in the mud.

"I can imagine what he said, your father." Her eyes glistened for the cow's endurance. For the fact that she would never know her own calf. The calf sprung out of the womb and into the boy's hands as though it welcomed this invasion, this strange freedom. It stood in the ankle-deep mud and shook all over.

"Start rubbing him with straw." The boy started to walk away.

"Wait a minute," she said weakly. "Are you just leaving the cow here to die? What will happen to the calf?"

"You hand feed it; he'll grow slower maybe. It's only a bull calf anyway."

"But I'm leaving tomorrow. I told you I wanted to go. I have to go tomorrow. Please." She looked at the boy's back as he turned away once more. His shoulders were set as though he was angry.

The boy turned around and looked at her, not shy any longer, but sizing her up. Testing her. "You know what my father said? He said you'd only go away one day and get married anyway and then the price of the land would be higher."

Could he see her crying? Could he hear her uneven feathery breathing? That she was afraid? The calf she was rubbing was struggling to nurse from his dying mother. She felt beads of sweat on her forehead, heat and tightness, as though she might throw up. "And you believe him, don't you?" She tried to lift the calf and carry him to the house. She felt her shoulders ache as she held the dangling animal high up against her face, leaning back with the awkward weight. As she passed by the boy, she hated him for all the times he'd stood back and watched.

"You can go then," she hissed. "Your father will start to bellow for you, and God damn him, I'll shout back tonight. Fuck you, I'll scream, fuck you for buying my dream and —"

The boy looked startled, shy again. He smiled a little though when she slipped in the mud and her arms gave the calf back to the ground again in a heap. As she went to lift the calf once more, the boy took him easily and quietly from her.

"I'll take him home. You have to leave tomorrow morning. But leave early before my father comes over to collect the rent. I'll say you weren't home, that you were working at the bar tonight."

"What about her?" She nodded toward the cow.

The boy was giving her an odd look. She imagined what he saw; the young woman, his neighbour, part-naked by the pump each night, the indecent one, covered with the slime of birth. Shivering for the way things had turned out.

"She won't live until morning. She's an old cow. This was her last calf."

She sighed. She'd seen enough shooting for one day, and had imagined even more. She wouldn't ask him to come back, take the gun from the side of the road, hold it steady and release the cow from where she was caught, somewhere between living and dying. The sound of the shotgun might bring the old man running and shouting. She sighed; there would be no gun, no mercy. Only one last look at the boy's young body holding the calf so firmly, like a farewell. The calf he held reminded her somewhat, in his white crown and wide eyes, of the boy. "Blanket over her?"

"If you want," and he smiled.

He walked ahead of her in the deep grass by the creek and when she could no longer see him, just hear his heavy walk growing lighter in the distance, she said softly, "I probably couldn't have raised the money for the place anyway."

The next morning the car was loaded so full behind that the shocks had seemingly given up and the tires looked somehow flatter than they should for such a long haul. Along the north shore of Superior, too. Some long climbs before the prairies. What could she leave behind? The books, some of the books. She would leave a box or two for the Dutch boys. Some of the stuff she'd read as a romantic nineteen-year-old travelling somewhere in Europe. *The Magus, Sexus, Le Grand Meaulnes.* She didn't feel involved with those stories any longer. Men-and-women stories. She would leave them all behind.

She would leave them in a conspicuous place in the barn where the brothers would be sure to check for signs of her defeat on the farm, signs that she'd idled and longed for marriage, instead of working. That's what they would be looking for and she would satisfy them. She'd let them think she curled up pretty as a girl on a calendar, the kind that fluttered hopelessly in their old man's barn. She would let them imagine that she lay there many a warm afternoon and just read. Finally falling asleep, some story of men and women open in her lap. The pale pages holding out the equally pale promise of falling in love. On an island in the Aegean, in a dance hall, or in a lost domain never found again after youth, the message was always the same. Love came swiftly and with certainty; one could always recognize it by its rightness. By its decency.

Had she been living a part in any one of those stories it would have been simple enough; the woman on the farm would have earned one of the neighbour's sons through her struggle for identity and independence, and the inevitable sexual encounter would have led sweetly to marriage, an honourable old age filled with children and memories. Yes, that's the way the readers would have it, she thought. And yet she thought of the pioneer woman, of the bones of her children lying beneath the ground, her memories picked as clean as those small bones.

On the way back from the barn she wondered what kind of lovers they would have made, any one of the Dutch boys. But first you had to have slept with a few tenderly, she thought. First you had to have let a few good ones slip through your hands. And those three boys hadn't done that yet, she knew. That reassured her as she walked slowly past the pump, her eyes cast down to the ground.

About six or seven paces from the ditch in front of the house she found the gun. It lay perfectly hidden in a fringe of long grass, which had somehow not been trampled by the men last night. It was heavier than she expected, the handle curved and cool, somewhat like the handle of the water pump.

The cow was still alive, with the oatsacking over her moving gently in the pale light. The water and hay she'd carried to her as a grim truce in the night were still untouched. The cow looked shrunken down, an awkward shape.

She wondered how much harder she'd become in just one night, how impatient she'd become to use the gun. Her short sleep before dawn filled with strange dreams of men coming to her for water, standing by the pump and pumping, pumping, pumping, the water never coming out of the ground, and then the dream of sewing up a dark wound, miles long, and the long, fine hairs from her head that she used as thread, constantly breaking. She ran a hand over her hair, feeling its strength, pulling it back from her scalp. And then she pointed the heavy gun, pulled the trigger. Never hearing the sound it made at all, just the boy's horn, suddenly wailing across the lonely fields.

"So is that how you got the scar?" Dean asks gently.

Else remembers how the cow shuddered and was still at last. How the blood ran into the mud; it seemed to belong there, as though the earth were a heavier, more profound flesh. "No, my aim was perfect," she says. She pushes away the uneaten raw meat on her plate and murmurs, "I remember reassuring myself there were many ways to feel guilt, and there was only one way to hold a gun."

When she looks up she is surprised to see Dean crying, his eyes glistening, his cheeks wet. He seems to sense that the scar on her left knee is older even yet, possibly as old as childhood, that the story will have to be told over and over again until she gets it right. But he is not disappointed.

They decide to go then, Dean guiding her out into the dark

streets by the elbow. When a huge peak of snow sculpted by the wind slips off an awning above their heads, cascading over their shoulders, he tightens his grip on her arm. But she isn't irritated by his taking hold of her; suddenly she feels it isn't so much a case of the woman beside him needing protection, but possibly the world needing some shelter from her.

She starts up her bruised station wagon, the same one that turned away from the farm that morning, carrying its heavy burden west, and for a few minutes neither of them speaks. She is watching the lights of the street lamps flashing in a regular rhythm over Dean's face and he is smiling now, his eyes glossed over from tears. They are suddenly on the south side, the old car climbing the hill with a grinding noise, the sound being absorbed into the river valley falling away behind them.

"Where to? Where do you live now?"

"When you make a loop and don't want to jump in it, or through it, what do you do with it?" he asks, a shy grin spreading slowly through his dark beard. "How long do you have to do a trick before you get it so you never miss it in your life? How long will a man keep missing before he will turn to honest work? — from that 1928 book on rope tricks. The preface was by Will Rogers."

"Yeah, rope tricks appeal to me," she says, feeling she has misjudged him, somewhere before the bathtub. "I'll bet they're quiet and give you a wonderful sensation of control."

"It's funny I should remember that," Dean says. And then Dean surprises her by admitting he'd never even heard of Will Rogers or rope spinning, much less a woman named Sally Pride, until that day on the train — he simply picked the book up off a bench in the train station. And made the rest of it up when he met her.

She is so surprised she forgets to shift gears turning left onto a dark street that leads away from Saskatchewan Drive, and his hand pushes down gently on hers, helping her find second. He leaves his hand resting there until they run out of road, parking before the last house on the street which has somehow strayed into a vast ravine park.

Even though it is dark, she can see that the house they've stopped before is old, at least by Albertan standards. And she wonders why Dean has chosen a house weathered by thirty or more hard winters, its look of permanence seemingly baffled by several odd-looking dormers and balconies added on as afterthoughts. It seems a house that will require a lot of care; it has an untrimmed hedge, and a porch partly heaved from last year's heavy frosts and partly propped up with new timbers. There are no front steps.

"I'd invite you inside, but as you can see I have to finish renovating before I can have any friends over. Right now I'm going in a back window, using the window box as the back stoop." He is backing through a gutter filled with drifting snow, leaving footprints that seem to be coming out of nowhere.

She tells him he should have asked her first, before he bought a run-down house, that the past is her strong point. And he murmurs then, his eyes especially green, that she would have said no for all the wrong reasons. And she knows their argument is over.